The Alpha's Healer

The Alpha's Healer: A Werewolf Shifter Romance

Copyright © 2024 by Alicia Hudson

All rights reserved. This book or any portion thereof may not be reproduced or used in any manner whatsoever without the express written permission of the publisher except for the use of brief quotations in a book review.

This is a work of fiction. Names, characters, events, places, and incidents are either the product of the author's imagination or used in a fictitious manner. Any resemblance to actual person, living or dead, or actual events is purely coincidental.

The Alpha's Healer

A Werewolf Shifter Romance

Alicia Hudson

CONTENTS

PROLOGUE	4
CHAPTER 1	9
CHAPTER 2	16
CHAPTER 3	24
CHAPTER 4	33
CHAPTER 5	40
CHAPTER 6	49
CHAPTER 7	58
CHAPTER 8	67
CHAPTER 9	77
CHAPTER 10	84
CHAPTER 11	93
CHAPTER 12	103
CHAPTER 13	108
CHAPTER 14	117
CHAPTER 15	127
EPILOGUE	136

PROLOGUE

Blood dripped from ancient stone, each crimson drop igniting silver sparks as it struck the earth. The old shaman's fingers trembled as he traced the final rune, completing the circle that would protect his greatest secret – his only secret.

"Listen carefully, little wolf," he whispered, his voice rough as mountain granite. "They're coming."

Six-year-old Alana huddled deeper into the shadows of the cave, her small hands clutched around a leather-bound journal nearly as big as her chest. Outside, thunder cracked across the sky like breaking bones, and wind howled through the redwoods with the voice of a thousand wolves.

Remember what I taught you." The shaman – the only father she'd ever known – pressed his palm against the cave wall. Beneath his touch, symbols began to glow with an otherworldly light. "Your gift is not a curse, no matter what they say. It's hope."

Heavy boots crunched through the underbrush outside. Shadows moved across the cave's mouth, cast by torchlight and hatred.

"Found you, old man!" A voice like broken glass scraped through the night. "Did you really think you could hide the child forever?"

The shaman straightened, his ceremonial robes whispering against stone. Blood from the ritual ran down his arms in rivulets, but his voice remained steady. "She is not yours to claim, Malik. The prophecy is not yours to corrupt."

Alana pressed herself deeper into the alcove as more figures appeared at the cave's entrance. Their eyes gleamed with an unnatural amber light, their bodies rippling with barely contained power.

"The prophecy speaks of absolute power," Malik snarled. "Power to heal or power to destroy. Did you think we wouldn't notice? That we wouldn't smell it in her blood?" The shaman's laugh was soft, sad. "You see only what your greed allows. The prophecy speaks not of power to take, but power to give." He glanced back at Alana's hiding spot, his dark eyes filled with centuries of wisdom and moments of love. "Power born of choice, not force."

Lightning split the sky, illuminating the cave in harsh white flashes. In those strobing moments, Alana saw them clearly – the hunters who had tracked them across three states. Their bodies began to twist and change, bone cracking as they took on forms that belonged in nightmares.

"Last chance, old man." Malik's voice distorted as his jaw elongated into a muzzle. "Give us the girl, and your death will be quick."

The shaman raised his blood-covered hands. The symbols on the cave walls flared brighter, and power thrummed through the air like plucked harp strings. "Alana," he called softly, never taking his eyes off the transforming werewolves. "Remember the story of the first healer?"

"She-she learned to heal by choosing to love instead of hate," Alana whispered back, clutching the journal tighter. The pages seemed to pulse against her chest, warm and alive with secrets.

"Good girl." The shaman's smile was fierce and proud. "Your mother would be so proud of who you'll become."

The first wolf lunged. The shaman's power exploded outward in a wave of silver light. Alana squeezed her eyes shut, but couldn't block out the sounds – snarls, screams, the wet thud of bodies hitting stone.

'Run!" The shaman's voice cut through the chaos. "Follow the ley lines like I taught you. Find the place where the redwoods whisper and water sings. Your destiny awaits there."

Alana scrambled deeper into the cave, toward the hidden tunnel they'd prepared months ago. Behind her, she heard Malik's roar of rage, the shaman's defiant chant, the sound of power meeting power in ancient combat.

The last thing she saw, before the tunnel's darkness swallowed her whole, was her father figure silhouetted against the storm-torn sky, his blood-painted hands holding back a tide of shadows and teeth.

The journal pressed against her heart like a promise as she ran into the darkness, its pages containing prophecies she couldn't yet read, power she couldn't yet understand. Tears froze on her cheeks as the storm raged above, but her feet kept moving, guided by the silver threads of power she could feel humming beneath the earth.

Behind her, a wolf's howl cut off mid-cry, and something ancient and powerful shook the very foundations of the mountain. The tunnel walls wept with condensation, each drop igniting with the same silver sparks as her guardian's blood.

Somewhere ahead lay her destiny — a pack, a purpose, a love that would change the very nature of power. But for now, there was only the darkness, the rumble of thunder, and the whispered echoes of her guardian's last lesson:

"The greatest power, little wolf, lies not in the healing of flesh, but in the courage to keep your heart open when the world would have you close it. Remember that. Remember me. Run."

And so she ran, carrying prophecy and power into the storm-torn night while behind her, the mountain shook with the death of old magic and the birth of something new.

The hunt had begun...

CHAPTER 1

*T*he fog hung thick and heavy, a spectral veil draped over the ancient redwoods. Through this misty shroud, a figure stumbled, her ragged breaths piercing the eerie silence of the forest. Alana's heart thundered in her chest, a frantic drumbeat echoing the pounding of her bare feet against the damp earth. Behind her, unseen but ever-present, the shadows of her pursuers loomed.

The forest seemed to whisper around her, the towering trees creaking and groaning like old men settling into their chairs. Alana's senses, heightened by fear and exhaustion, picked up every snapping twig, every rustle of leaves. Each sound sent a jolt of terror through her already trembling body.

Her lungs burned, desperate for air, but she dared not slow her pace. The coppery taste of blood filled her mouth, a grim reminder of the injuries she'd sustained in her desperate flight. Her tattered clothes, once pristine and white, now bore the angry red stains of her ordeal.

As she ran, memories flashed through her mind like a fevered dream. The peaceful solitude of her mentor's cabin, shattered by the arrival of them

The hunger in their eyes as they spoke of prophecies and power. The sickening realization that she was no longer safe in the only home she'd ever known.

A root, gnarled and treacherous, caught Alana's foot. She stumbled, her world tilting sideways as she crashed to the forest floor. Pain exploded through her body, stealing what little breath remained in her lungs. For a moment, she lay there, the damp earth cool against her flushed cheek.

Get up! Her mind screamed, even as her body protested. *They're coming!*

With a groan that was part pain, part determination, Alana forced herself to her feet. Her legs trembled beneath her, threatening to give way at any moment. She pressed a hand to her side, feeling the warm stickiness of fresh blood seeping through her fingers.

The sound of rushing water reached her ears, growing louder with each stumbling step. Hope, fragile as a butterfly's wing, fluttered in her chest. Water meant life, meant a chance to throw off her pursuers.

Alana pushed through a thick curtain of ferns, emerging onto a rocky ledge. Before her, a majestic waterfall cascaded down a sheer cliff face, its roar drowning out even the frantic beating of her heart. The mist rising from the churning pool at its base softened the harsh edges of the world, lending an almost dreamlike quality to the scene.

For a brief moment, Alana stood transfixed by the raw beauty before her. Then, reality came crashing back as a howl echoed through the forest behind her. It was a sound that sent ice through her veins, primal and hungry.

Her legs gave way beneath her, and Alana collapsed to her knees on the mossy stone. Exhaustion and blood loss conspired against her, pulling her down into a swirling vortex of darkness. As consciousness slipped away, her last thoughts were of the gentle shaman who had raised her, and the mysterious power that now seemed more curse than gift.

The last thing Alana saw before the world faded to black was a pair of golden eyes, gleaming from the shadows at the edge of the clearing. Then, mercifully, oblivion claimed her.

****

The crunch of gravel underfoot broke the stillness of the forest. Beta Liam raised a hand, halting his patrol. His nostrils flared, catching the metallic tang of blood on the misty air.

"There," he growled, pointing towards the waterfall. "Someone's hurt."

The patrol moved silently, melting into the shadows of the ancient redwoods. As they approached the clearing, Liam's eyes narrowed, focusing on the crumpled form near the water's edge.

"It's a woman," whispered Keira, the youngest of the group. "Is she...?"

"Alive," Liam confirmed, kneeling beside the unconscious figure. His fingers pressed against her neck, feeling the weak flutter of a pulse. "Barely."

The woman's clothes were torn and bloodied, her skin pale beneath a layer of dirt and bruises. Liam's brow furrowed as he took in her injuries.

"She's not one of ours," growled Darius, his hand instinctively moving to the knife at his belt. "Could be a trap."

Liam shook his head. "No Pack scent on her. She's human... or something else." He scooped the woman into his arms, her body limp as a rag doll. "Whatever she is, she needs help. We're taking her back to the village."

"But the Alpha-" Keira started.

"I'll deal with Rafe," Liam cut her off. "Now move. She doesn't have much time."

The patrol melted back into the forest, moving swiftly through paths known only to them. As they approached the hidden entrance to Whispering Falls, the roar of the waterfall grew louder.

Liam barked out a command, and two young wolves guarding the entrance snapped to attention. Their eyes widened at the sight of the unconscious woman in his arms.

"Alert the healers," Liam ordered. "And find the Alpha. Now!"

The hidden village of Whispering Falls bustled with activity as word of the stranger spread. Curious eyes peered from windows and doorways as Liam carried Alana through the winding paths between rustic cabins and towering redwoods.

At the village center, a crowd had already gathered. Whispers rippled through the assembly like wind through leaves.

"Who is she?"

"Where did she come from?"

"Is it safe to bring her here?"

The crowd parted as Rafe, Alpha of the Redwood Pack, strode forward. His golden eyes, so like those Alana had seen before losing consciousness, now blazed with a mixture of concern and suspicion.

"What's the meaning of this, Liam?" he demanded, his voice a low rumble that sent shivers through the gathered pack members.

Liam met his Alpha's gaze steadily. "Found her by the falls, Rafe. She's hurt bad. Human, as far as I can tell, but..." He hesitated, lowering his voice. "There's something different about her. A scent I can't place."

Rafe's nostrils flared as he leaned in, inhaling deeply. His eyes widened almost imperceptibly before his face settled back into a mask of neutrality.

"Take her to the healing den," he ordered, his tone brooking no argument. "Mara will tend to her."

As Liam moved to obey, a voice rang out from the crowd. "We can't trust her!" All eyes turned to Lysandra, her beautiful features twisted with disdain. "She could be a spy from the Shadow Pack!"

Murmurs of agreement rippled through the gathering. Rafe silenced them with a growl, his eyes flashing dangerously.

"Enough!" he snapped. "She'll be guarded until we know more. But we don't turn away those in need. That's not our way."

His gaze swept the crowd, challenging anyone to disagree. None did.

As Liam carried Alana towards the healing den, her eyelids fluttered. For a brief moment, her eyes opened, locking onto Rafe's. In that instant, something passed between them – a jolt of recognition, a spark of connection that defied explanation.

Then Alana's eyes rolled back, and she slipped once more into unconsciousness.

Rafe watched them go, his face unreadable. But beneath the surface, turmoil raged. Who was this stranger? And why did he feel as though her arrival had set in motion events that would change everything?

CHAPTER 2

The morning mist clung to the towering redwoods like gossamer veils, transforming Whispering Falls into an ethereal realm caught between worlds. Alana stood at the edge of the training grounds, her fingers absently tracing the rough bark of an ancient tree. The past week had been a whirlwind of wary glances and hushed whispers, the pack's suspicion a tangible force that set her nerves on edge.

Before her, a group of young werewolves sparred under the watchful eye of Beta Liam. Their movements were a blur of sinewy grace, punctuated by grunts of exertion and the occasional yelp of pain. Alana's gaze was drawn to one wolf in particular – a lanky youth with tousled brown hair and eager eyes.

"Come on, Caleb!" Liam's voice boomed across the clearing. "You're telegraphing your moves. Finn can read you like a book!"

Caleb's face screwed up in concentration as he circled his opponent. Finn, a cockier boy with a mop of unruly red hair, grinned wickedly. "Yeah, Caleb," he taunted, his voice carrying a hint of a growl. "Why don't you just write your next move on your forehead?"

Something in Finn's tone made Alana's skin prickle. There was an edge there, sharper than mere competition. As Caleb lunged forward, Finn's eyes flashed with a predatory gleam.

What happened next seemed to unfold in slow motion. Finn sidestepped Caleb's attack with unnatural speed, then brought his elbow down hard on the smaller boy's back. The crack of impact echoed through the clearing like a gunshot.

Caleb hit the ground with a sickening thud, his body twisting at an unnatural angle. A scream of agony tore from his throat, raw and primal.

"Caleb!" Liam's roar shook the very trees as he bounded across the clearing.

But Alana was already moving. Her feet carried her forward of their own accord, the world around her fading to a muted blur. All she could see was Caleb, his face contorted in pain, his leg bent at an impossible angle.

She dropped to her knees beside him, heedless of the growls and snarls erupting around her. Caleb's eyes, wild with pain and fear, locked onto hers.

"It hurts," he whimpered, his voice small and broken. "Make it stop. Please."

Something ancient and powerful stirred within Alana, a force as old as the earth itself. Her hands moved of their own volition, coming to rest on Caleb's twisted leg.

"Shh," she murmured, her voice taking on a lyrical quality that seemed to resonate with the very air around them. "Be still, little wolf. Let the earth's wisdom flow through you."

A warmth began to build beneath her palms, pulsing in time with Caleb's ragged breaths. The air around them seemed to shimmer, as if reality itself was bending to Alana's will.

Gasps of astonishment rippled through the gathered crowd as Caleb's leg began to straighten, the swelling visibly receding. The boy's whimpers of pain gave way to sighs of relief.

Alana's world narrowed to a pinpoint of concentration, every fiber of her being focused on channeling the healing energy coursing through her. She could feel Caleb's bones knitting together, his torn muscles mending, his pain ebbing away like the tide.

When at last she lifted her hands, they trembled with exhaustion. Caleb stared up at her in wide-eyed wonder, flexing his newly-healed leg as if he couldn't quite believe it was real.

"How...?" he breathed, his voice barely above a whisper.

The silence that had fallen over the clearing was shattered by a single word, spoken in a voice that sent shivers down Alana's spine.

"Impossible."

She turned to find Rafe standing at the edge of the clearing, his golden eyes blazing with an intensity that stole her breath away. In that moment, as their gazes locked, Alana knew that everything had changed.

The gift she had hidden for so long was now laid bare for all to see. And in the depths of Rafe's eyes, she saw a maelstrom of emotions – wonder, fear, and something else, something that made her heart race in a way that had nothing to do with her healing magic.

As the pack erupted into a cacophony of exclamations and questions, Alana remained kneeling beside Caleb, suddenly aware of the weight of destiny settling upon her shoulders. The winds of change were blowing through Whispering Falls, and she stood at the eye of the storm.

****

The clearing erupted into chaos, a cacophony of voices rising and falling like waves crashing against a rocky shore. Alana remained frozen in place, her hands still tingling with residual energy, as the pack members surged around her in a whirlwind of motion and sound.

"Did you see that?"

"It's not possible!"

"She healed him with just a touch!"

Caleb scrambled to his feet, testing his newly-healed leg with cautious steps. His eyes were wide with wonder as he turned to Alana. "It doesn't hurt at all," he marveled, bouncing on the balls of his feet. "It's like it never happened!"

Before Alana could respond, a firm hand gripped her arm, pulling her to her feet. She found herself face to face with Rafe, his golden eyes boring into hers with an intensity that made her breath catch in her throat.

"What are you?" he demanded, his voice low and rough with barely contained emotion. The subtle growl underlying his words sent shivers down Alana's spine.

She opened her mouth to reply, but the words died on her tongue as the crowd parted like water around a stone. A hush fell over the clearing as Elder Elara stepped forward, her silver hair gleaming in the dappled sunlight that filtered through the canopy.

The pack's healer moved with a grace that belied her advanced years, her eyes — a startling shade of violet — fixed on Alana with laser-like focus. As she approached, the air seemed to crackle with an ancient power that made the hairs on the back of Alana's neck stand on end.

"Well, well," Elara murmured, her voice carrying clearly despite its soft one. "It seems the winds of change have indeed blown something extraordinary into our midst."

She circled Alana slowly, her gaze roving over the younger woman with unabashed curiosity. "Tell me, child," she said, coming to a stop before Alana. "Where did you learn such magic?"

Alana swallowed hard, acutely aware of the dozens of eyes fixed upon her. "I... I've always been able to do it," she stammered, her voice barely above a whisper. "My mentor – the shaman who raised me – he helped me understand it, control it."

A murmur rippled through the crowd at her words. Elara's eyes narrowed thoughtfully. "A shaman, you say? Interesting. Very interesting indeed."

Rafe stepped forward, his presence a palpable force at Alana's side. "Elder Elara," he began, but the old woman cut him off with a sharp gesture.

"Not now, Alpha," she said, her tone brooking no argument. "This is a matter that requires... delicate handling." Her gaze swept over the assembled pack members, lips pursed in disapproval at their open gawking. "This is not a spectacle for idle gossip. Return to your duties, all of you."

There was a moment of hesitation before the pack began to disperse, casting backward glances and whispered comments as they went. Soon, only Rafe, Elara, and a still-awestruck Caleb remained with Alana in the clearing.

Elara turned her attention back to Alana, her expression softening slightly. "Come with me, child," she said, extending a gnarled hand. "We have much to discuss."

As Alana reached out to take the offered hand, Rafe's voice cut through the air like a steel blade. "Wait." His hand came to rest on Alana's shoulder, the heat of his touch searing through the thin fabric of her shirt. "I need answers, Elara. What does this mean for the pack?"

The elder's violet eyes flashed with a mixture of amusement and exasperation. "It means, my dear Alpha, that the Great Spirit has seen fit to bless us in ways we cannot yet fathom." She fixed Rafe with a pointed stare. "Unless, of course, you'd prefer to question such a gift?"

Rafe's jaw clenched, a muscle ticking visibly as he wrestled with his thoughts. After a long moment, he gave a curt nod. "Very well. But I want to be present for this... discussion."

"As you wish," Elara conceded with a small smile. She turned, beckoning Alana to follow. "Come. My cottage will offer us the privacy we need."

As they made their way through the village, Alana could feel the weight of countless stares upon her. Whispers followed in their wake like autumn leaves skittering across the forest floor. She kept her eyes fixed on Elara's back, trying to ignore the growing knot of anxiety in her stomach.

Rafe's presence at her side was both comforting and unsettling, his proximity sending sparks of awareness skittering across her skin. She risked a glance at him from the corner of her eye, only to find his gaze already fixed upon her, his expression unreadable.

As they approached a small cottage nestled against the base of a massive redwood, Elara paused, turning to face Alana once more. "Tell me, child," she said, her voice taking on a lyrical quality that seemed to resonate with the very air around them. "Are you ready to embrace your destiny?"

The question hung in the air between them, heavy with the weight of untold possibilities. Alana drew in a deep breath, feeling as though she stood on the precipice of a great change. With a single word, she knew, she would be stepping into a future both thrilling and terrifying in its potential.

"Yes," she whispered, her voice growing stronger as she repeated, "Yes, I am."

Elara's answering smile was as enigmatic as it was knowing. "Then let us begin," she said, pushing open the cottage door. "For the path that lies before you, Alana, is one that will shape not only your fate, but the fate of us all."

CHAPTER 3

The ancient redwoods loomed overhead, their branches interlocking like gnarled fingers against the twilight sky. Rafe stood at the edge of the clearing, his powerful frame as still as the centuries-old sentinels surrounding him. Only his eyes betrayed his inner turmoil, golden irises tracking Alana's every move as she tended to a young pack member's scraped knee.

Her hands glowed with a soft, ethereal light that seemed to pulse in time with the forest's heartbeat. The child's whimpers faded to sighs of relief as the angry red scratch knitted itself closed under Alana's gentle touch.

Rafe's nostrils flared, drinking in her scent – a intoxicating blend of wild herbs and something else, something ancient and powerful that made his wolf stir restlessly beneath his skin. His claws itched to emerge, every instinct screaming at him to claim, to possess.

But doubt gnawed at him like a hungry wolf, its teeth sharp and unrelenting.

"You're staring again," Liam's gruff voice cut through Rafe's reverie. His Beta materialized at his side, following his gaze to where Alana now stood, smiling as the healed child scampered off to rejoin his playmates.

Rafe's jaw clenched, a low growl rumbling in his chest. "I'm observing," he corrected, the words coated with a layer of frost. "There's a difference."

Liam arched an eyebrow, a hint of amusement dancing in his eyes. "Is there? Because from where I'm standing, it looks an awful lot like our mighty Alpha is..." He paused, savoring the moment. "Mooning."

Rafe's head snapped around, his eyes flashing dangerously. "Choose your next words carefully, old friend," he warned, a hint of fang peeking through his snarl.

Liam raised his hands in mock surrender, but the smirk never left his face. "All I'm saying is, you've been watching her like a hawk for weeks now. Don't you think it's time you actually talked to her? Find out what she's really about?"

Rafe turned back to the clearing, his gaze once again drawn to Alana like a lodestone to true north. She moved with a grace that seemed almost otherworldly, her copper hair catching the last rays of sunlight like living flame.

"It's not that simple," Rafe muttered, his voice low enough that only Liam's enhanced hearing could catch it. "Her power... it's unlike anything I've ever seen. How do we know we can trust her? That she won't turn on us the moment it suits her?"

As if sensing his scrutiny, Alana looked up, her emerald eyes locking with Rafe's across the clearing. For a heartbeat that seemed to stretch into eternity, the world fell away. Rafe felt a jolt of... something... course through him, electric and terrifying in its intensity.

Alana's lips parted, as if to speak, but before she could, a commotion erupted at the edge of the village. Rafe tore his gaze away, every muscle tensing as the scent of blood and fear sliced through the air.

"Hunters!" The cry went up, sending a ripple of panic through the gathered pack members. "Hunters in the forest!"

In an instant, Rafe's doubts and conflicted emotions were shoved aside, buried beneath the weight of his duty as Alpha. He strode forward, his voice ringing out with the authority of a born leader.

"Liam, gather the warriors. Elena, get the pups to the safe house. Now!"

As the pack scrambled to obey, Rafe's eyes sought out Alana once more. She stood frozen in place, her face pale with shock and fear. For a moment, uncertainty flickered in her eyes, and Rafe felt a stab of something dangerously close to disappointment.

But then her spine straightened, determination hardening her delicate features into a mask of resolve. She stepped forward, her voice clear and steady as she called out, "I can help. Let me help."

Rafe hesitated, warring instincts tearing at him. The Alpha in him snarled at the idea of putting an outsider — a potential threat — in the middle of pack business. But something deeper, something primal that he couldn't quite name, whispered that turning away her aid would be a grave mistake.

In the end, it was the memory of Caleb's miraculously healed leg that decided him. He gave a sharp nod, beckoning her forward. "Stay close," he ordered, his voice rough with suppressed emotion. "And Alana?" Their eyes met once more, and this time Rafe allowed a hint of the turmoil roiling within him to show. "Don't make me regret this."

As they raced towards the sounds of battle, Rafe couldn't shake the feeling that he was hurtling towards a crossroads — one that would change not just his life, but the fate of his entire pack. And at the center of it all stood Alana, a mystery wrapped in power and grace, holding the key to a future he couldn't begin to fathom.

The forest seemed to hold its breath, waiting to see what choice the Alpha would make. For in that moment, balanced on the knife's edge between trust and suspicion, lay the seeds of a destiny that would reshape their world forever.

****

The great hall of the Redwood Pack thrummed with tension, dozens of eyes fixed on the towering figure of their Alpha. Rafe stood at the head of the long wooden table, his hands splayed on its surface, claws just barely peeking through. The flickering light from the hearth cast dancing shadows across his face, lending him an almost preternatural air.

Alana stood before him, her chin raised defiantly despite the slight tremor in her hands. The pack formed a loose circle around them, their whispers a low, constant susurration like wind through leaves.

Rafe's voice cut through the murmurs, silencing them instantly. "You understand the gravity of what I'm proposing?" His golden eyes bored into Alana's, searching for any hint of deception.

Alana met his gaze steadily. "I do," she replied, her voice clear and unwavering. "I'm to remain here, under the supervision of Elder Elara and the pack. My abilities are to be used for the benefit of the Redwood Pack, and I'm not to leave the territory without express permission."

A muscle ticked in Rafe's jaw. "And you agree to these terms?"

"I do," Alana repeated, then added softly, "Thank you for this chance, Alpha."

Rafe's nostrils flared, drinking in her scent. For a moment, something flickered in his eyes — a heat that made Alana's breath catch in her throat. But it was gone as quickly as it appeared, replaced by the cool mask of authority.

"Very well," he growled, straightening to his full, imposing height. "Elder Elara, I trust you'll oversee her training and... integration."

The silver-haired woman stepped forward, her violet eyes twinkling with barely suppressed amusement. "It would be my pleasure, Alpha," she said, laying a gnarled hand on Alana's arm. "Come, child. We have much to discuss."

As Elara led Alana towards the exit, the pack parted before them like water around stones. Alana could feel the weight of their stares, a mixture of curiosity, wariness, and in some cases, outright hostility.

Just as they reached the door, Rafe's voice rang out once more. "Alana."

She turned, finding him suddenly much closer than she expected. His presence seemed to fill the entire room, making it hard to breathe.

"Remember," he said, his voice low enough that only she and Elara could hear, "I'll be watching. One misstep, one hint that you're a threat to this pack, and our agreement is void. Are we clear?"

Alana swallowed hard, fighting the urge to step back. "Crystal," she managed, her voice barely above a whisper.

Something that might have been approval flashed in Rafe's eyes. He nodded once, then turned on his heel, striding back to the head of the table.

As Elara ushered her out into the cool night air, Alana let out a shaky breath she hadn't realized she'd been holding.

"Well now," Elara chuckled, patting Alana's arm. "That was certainly... invigorating."

Alana shot her a bewildered look. "Invigorating? I felt like I was being dissected."

Elara's laughter rang out, clear and bright in the darkness. "Oh, my dear. You have no idea the effect you're having on our stoic Alpha. It's been a long time since I've seen Rafe so... unsettled."

Before Alana could respond, a figure melted out of the shadows, resolving into the lithe form of a woman with hair like spun moonlight. Lysandra, Alana's mind supplied, recalling the she-wolf's cold stare from earlier encounters.

"So," Lysandra drawled, her voice dripping with false sweetness, "the little witch gets to stay. How... quaint."

Elara's grip on Alana's arm tightened warningly. "Mind your tongue, Lysandra," the elder said, her tone sharp. "Alana is here by the Alpha's decree. Or do you question Rafe's judgment?"

Lysandra's eyes narrowed, but she took a step back. "Of course not, Elder," she said, her smile not quite reaching her eyes. "I was merely... welcoming our new packmate."

With a final, calculating look at Alana, Lysandra melted back into the shadows.

Elara sighed, shaking her head. "Pay her no mind, child. Come, let's get you settled. Tomorrow, your real work begins."

As they made their way through the moonlit village, Alana couldn't shake the feeling of being watched. She glanced back at the great hall, its windows glowing with warm light.

For just a moment, she caught a glimpse of a tall figure silhouetted against the glow – broad-shouldered and undeniably powerful. Even at this distance, she could feel the intensity of Rafe's gaze, sending a shiver down her spine that had nothing to do with the cool night air.

Alana turned away quickly, hurrying to keep pace with Elara. But she couldn't escape the certainty that, one way or another, her life had changed irrevocably. The path ahead was shrouded in mist, full of unknown dangers and possibilities.

And at the center of it all stood Rafe, the Alpha whose golden eyes seemed to see right through to her very soul. Alana squared her shoulders, determination settling over her like a cloak. Whatever challenges lay ahead, she would face them head-on.

For in the depths of those piercing eyes, beyond the wariness and the intensity, she had glimpsed something else – a flicker of connection that called to something wild and ancient within her own heart.

CHAPTER 4

*T*he shadows lengthened across Blackrock Ridge as twilight painted the sky in hues of bruised purple and blood orange. Zev, Alpha of the Shadow Pack, stood atop a jagged outcropping, his scarred face a mask of stone as he gazed out over his domain. The wind whispered through the sparse, twisted pines, carrying with it the scent of decay and desperation that had become all too familiar in recent moons.

A twig snapped behind him, and Zev's ears twitched. He didn't turn, knowing only one wolf would dare approach him uninvited. "Speak, Koran," he growled, his voice low and guttural, like gravel scraping against bone.

Koran, a wiry beta with eyes that gleamed like polished obsidian, slunk forward. "Alpha," he began, his words tumbling out in an eager rush, "our spies bring news from Whispering Falls. The Redwood Pack shelters a healer of... extraordinary ability."

Zev's muscles coiled beneath his skin, tension rippling through his massive frame like a gathering storm. "Extraordinary how?" he demanded, finally turning to face his beta. The scar that bisected his left eye seemed to pulse in the fading light, a testament to past battles and unquenched thirst for vengeance.

Koran licked his lips, tasting the significance of his words before speaking them aloud. "They say she can mend wounds with a touch, ease pain with a whisper. Animals bend to her will, and..." he hesitated, then plunged on, "some whisper that she communes with spirits of the forest itself."

A low, rumbling growl built in Zev's chest, a sound that sent shivers down Koran's spine and set the nearby pines to trembling. The Alpha's eyes blazed with a feral light, reflecting the dying sun like twin infernos. "A healer," he breathed, the words hanging in the air like smoke. "At last."

Memories flashed through Zev's mind, unbidden and unwelcome. The seer's wizened face, her milky eyes unseeing yet piercing his very soul as she croaked out the prophecy that had haunted him for years. *"Shadow will fall to tooth and claw, unless the one who mends becomes your law."* The words had been etched into his heart, driving every decision, every ruthless act since that fateful day.

"Her name?" Zev demanded, his voice sharp as a blade.

"Alana," Koran supplied quickly. "She arrived recently, seeking refuge. The Redwood Alpha, Rafe, has taken a... particular interest in her."

Zev's lips curled back in a snarl, revealing fangs that gleamed wickedly in the twilight. "Has he now?" he mused, his tone deceptively soft. "How... predictable."

He turned back to the vista before him, drinking in the harsh beauty of his territory. The Shadow Pack's lands were unforgiving, a reflection of the wolves who called it home. But for too long, they had been barely surviving, their numbers dwindling, their strength waning. This healer, this Alana, could change everything.

"Prepare the pack," Zev commanded, his voice ringing with authority that brooked no argument. "We move at midnight."

Koran's eyes widened. "But Alpha, surely we need more time to—"

Zev whirled, faster than thought, his hand closing around Koran's throat. He lifted the beta effortlessly, bringing him close enough to feel the heat of his breath. "You question me?" he hissed, his eyes flashing dangerously.

"N-no, Alpha," Koran choked out, clawing uselessly at the iron grip around his neck.

Zev held him there a moment longer, savoring the fear that radiated from his beta in waves, before dropping him unceremoniously to the ground. Koran gasped for air, rubbing his bruised throat as he scrambled backward.

"Midnight," Zev repeated, his tone brooking no further argument. "We will take what is rightfully ours. The Shadow Pack will rise again, and this healer..." A slow, predatory smile spread across his face, made all the more terrifying by the scar that twisted it into something grotesque. "This Alana will be the key to our ascension."

As Koran stumbled away to relay the orders, Zev turned his gaze once more to the darkening sky. The first stars were beginning to appear, cold and distant, indifferent to the machinations of wolves below. But Zev's blood sang with anticipation, with the thrill of the hunt to come.

"Soon," he whispered to the encroaching night, his words a vow and a threat wrapped into one. "Soon, little healer, you will be mine. And with you by my side, no force in this world will stand against the Shadow Pack."

The wind picked up, carrying his words away into the gathering gloom. In the distance, a lone wolf howled, the sound mournful and filled with portent. The pieces were in motion, the board set. And as full darkness descended upon Blackrock Ridge, Zev, Alpha of the Shadow Pack, prepared to make his move in a game where the stakes were nothing less than the fate of all werewolves.

****

Zev's claws raked across the ancient oak table, leaving deep gouges in the weathered wood. Maps and scrolls littered its surface, illuminated by guttering candles that cast dancing shadows across the war room of the Shadow Pack's den. The Alpha's eyes, gleaming with a feverish light, darted between the documents, his mind racing with possibilities.

"Malik," he barked, not bothering to look up as his most trusted strategist entered the room. "Tell me about the Redwood Pack's defenses."

Malik, a grizzled wolf with a notched ear and a perpetual scowl, approached the table. His voice was gravelly as he spoke, "Their territory is well-guarded, especially near the falls. The forest itself seems to work against intruders, roots rising to trip, branches swinging low to—"

Zev's fist slammed onto the table, sending scrolls flying. "I don't want excuses," he snarled. "I want solutions. How do we get to the healer?"

Malik's expression remained impassive, but a bead of sweat trickled down his temple. "We've identified a weak point here," he said, pointing to a spot on the map. "A ravine that cuts through their southeastern border. It's treacherous, but—"

"But nothing," Zev cut him off, a predatory grin spreading across his face. "Treacherous is exactly what we need. Prepare a strike team. We move in three days."

The strategist hesitated, his fingers drumming nervously on the hilt of the dagger at his hip. "Alpha, with all due respect, shouldn't we gather more intelligence? We don't even know the full extent of this healer's powers, or how closely she's guarded."

Zev whirled on him, moving with preternatural speed. In an instant, he had Malik pinned against the rough stone wall, forearm pressed against the wolf's throat. "You think I haven't considered every angle?" he hissed, his breath hot on Malik's face. "Every moment we delay is another moment our pack weakens. Another pup lost to illness, another warrior succumbing to wounds that won't heal."

He released Malik, who slumped against the wall, gasping. Zev stalked back to the table, his movements tightly coiled, like a spring about to release. "Besides," he continued, his voice dropping to a low rumble, "we have an ace up our sleeve."

With a flick of his wrist, Zev produced a small, intricately carved wooden box. He opened it, revealing a shimmering green powder that seemed to pulse with its own inner light. Malik's eyes widened in recognition.

"Is that...?" he began, unable to finish the question.

Zev nodded, a cruel smile playing at the corners of his mouth. "Dreamshade. Extremely rare, extremely potent. One pinch of this, and even the mightiest Alpha will be lost in hallucinations, unable to distinguish friend from foe."

He snapped the box shut, the sound echoing in the chamber like a death knell. "We'll use it to create a diversion. While Rafe and his inner circle are trapped in their own minds, we'll slip in and take what's ours."

Malik straightened, a newfound respect—and fear—evident in his eyes. "And the healer? What if she resists?"

Zev's laugh was cold and mirthless. "Oh, she'll resist. They always do. But in the end, she'll see things our way." He turned back to the maps, his fingers tracing the path they would take. "After all, what choice will she have when the lives of her precious new pack hang in the balance?"

The Alpha's eyes glazed over, lost in a vision of the future. "Can you imagine it, Malik? Our pack, stronger than ever. No more watching our young waste away. No more agonizing deaths from battle wounds. With her by our side, we'll be unstoppable."

Malik nodded slowly, caught up in the fervor of Zev's words. "And the prophecy? You believe she's the one?"

Zev's hand unconsciously rose to the scar that marred his face, a reminder of past failures and the weight of destiny. "She has to be," he murmured, more to himself than to Malik. Then, louder, "Gather the others. We have much to prepare."

As Malik hurried from the room, Zev turned to face the single window, cut high into the stone wall. The waning moon cast its pale light across the desolate landscape of Blackrock Ridge. In three days' time, that same moon would witness the fruition of his plans.

"Soon, little healer," he whispered to the night. "Soon, you'll understand. The Shadow Pack's survival is worth any price. And I..." His eyes flashed alpha red in the darkness. "I am prepared to pay it."

The wind howled outside, a mournful sound that seemed to carry a warning. But Zev paid it no heed. His course was set, his resolve unshakable. In three days, the fate of two packs would hang in the balance. And Zev intended to tip the scales in his favor, no matter the cost.

CHAPTER 5

The moon hung low and luminous over Whispering Falls, its silver light filtering through the mist-shrouded canopy of ancient redwoods. Alana moved through the forest like a wraith, her bare feet whispering against the moss-covered ground. The night air was thick with the scent of pine and damp earth, a primal perfume that seemed to awaken something deep within her.

She paused at the edge of a small clearing, her breath catching in her throat. There, bathed in moonlight, stood Rafe. The Alpha's powerful frame was silhouetted against the silvery backdrop, his muscles rippling beneath his skin like liquid steel. For a moment, Alana allowed herself to drink in the sight of him, her heart thundering in her chest like a caged bird.

Rafe turned, his eyes locking onto hers with an intensity that made her knees weak. "Alana," he growled, her name a low rumble that seemed to vibrate through the very air between them. "You shouldn't be out here alone."

She took a tentative step forward, drawn to him like a moth to flame. "I couldn't sleep," she murmured, her voice barely above a whisper. "The moon... it calls to me."

A look of understanding flickered across Rafe's face, softening the hard planes of his features. "I know that feeling well," he admitted, closing the distance between them with long, purposeful strides.

As he drew near, Alana could feel the heat radiating from his body, a stark contrast to the cool night air. Her skin prickled with awareness, every nerve ending suddenly alive and singing. She inhaled sharply, catching the musky scent of pine and something uniquely *Rafe* that made her head spin.

"We shouldn't—" Rafe began, but his words were cut short as a twig snapped in the darkness beyond the clearing. In an instant, he was in motion, pushing Alana behind him and facing the threat with a low, menacing growl.

A deer burst from the underbrush, startled by their presence. As it bounded away, Alana felt a bubble of nervous laughter rise in her throat. The tension of the moment shattered, leaving behind a charged silence.

Rafe turned back to her, his eyes blazing with an emotion Alana couldn't quite name. "This is dangerous," he said, his voice rough with restraint. "You don't know what you do to me, Alana."

She met his gaze unflinchingly, feeling a surge of boldness. "Maybe I want to find out," she whispered, reaching out to place a hand on his chest. Beneath her palm, she could feel the frantic beating of his heart, matching the rhythm of her own.

For a breathless moment, they stood frozen, teetering on the edge of something profound and irrevocable. Then, with a growl that was more animal than man, Rafe pulled her to him, crushing his lips to hers in a kiss that set her world ablaze.

Alana melted into him, her arms twining around his neck as she returned the kiss with equal fervor. It was like nothing she had ever experienced before — wild and primal, yet achingly tender. Rafe's hands roamed her back, leaving trails of fire in their wake, and she gasped against his mouth.

As suddenly as it had begun, Rafe tore himself away, putting distance between them. His chest heaved as he fought for control, his eyes flickering between their normal hazel and a lupine gold. "We can't," he said, his voice raw with regret and desire. "It's too dangerous. The pack, the prophecy... there's too much at stake."

Alana felt as though she'd been doused with ice water. Reality came crashing back, bringing with it the weight of their responsibilities and the looming threat of the Shadow Pack. "I... I understand," she managed, even as her heart ached with the lie.

Rafe's expression softened, and he reached out to cup her cheek gently. "Alana, you must know... if things were different—"

She placed her fingers against his lips, silencing him. "Don't," she pleaded. "Don't make promises we can't keep."

A howl echoed through the night, startling them both. Rafe's posture immediately changed, the Alpha reasserting itself as he scanned the treeline.

"We should head back," he said, all business once more. "It's not safe out here."

As they made their way back to the village, walking close but not touching, Alana couldn't shake the feeling that something fundamental had shifted between them. The air crackled with unspoken words and unfulfilled desires, a tension as palpable as the mist that swirled around their feet.

Back in the safety of Whispering Falls, they paused at the edge of the village. Rafe turned to her, his eyes searching her face as if committing it to memory. "Goodnight, Alana," he said softly, his voice carrying a wealth of meaning.

"Goodnight, Alpha," she replied, forcing herself to use his title as a reminder of the barriers between them.

As she watched him walk away, disappearing into the shadows of the village, Alana wrapped her arms around herself. The ghost of his kiss still lingered on her lips, a bittersweet reminder of what could never be. With a heavy heart, she turned towards her own quarters, knowing that sleep would elude her for the rest of the night.

Unbeknownst to either of them, a pair of jealous eyes had witnessed their moonlit encounter. Lysandra melted back into the shadows, her heart burning with rage and betrayal. As she slipped away to make contact with her true master, one thought consumed her: Zev would be very interested to learn of this development.

****

The first light of dawn barely penetrated the heavy curtains of Rafe's quarters as he paced the room, his bare feet silent on the wooden floor. Sleep had eluded him, his mind a maelstrom of conflicting emotions and responsibilities. The scent of Alana lingered on his skin, a constant reminder of their moonlit encounter.

A low growl escaped his throat as he ran his hands through his disheveled hair. The beast within him clawed at his insides, demanding to be unleashed, to claim what it saw as rightfully his. Rafe's eyes flashed gold as he fought to maintain control.

A knock at the door jolted him from his internal struggle. "Enter," he barked, his voice rough with fatigue and tension.

Liam, his Beta, stepped into the room, his brow furrowed with concern. "Alpha, the border patrols have reported increased activity from the Shadow Pack. We need to discuss our next move."

Rafe nodded curtly, grateful for the distraction. "Gather the council. I'll be there shortly."

As Liam turned to leave, he hesitated. "There's something else, Rafe," he said, dropping formalities. "The pack... they're talking. About you and the healer."

Rafe's jaw clenched, his shoulders tensing visibly. "What exactly are they saying, Liam?"

The Beta shifted uncomfortably. "Some think she's a distraction, a weakness. Others... they see how she affects you. How you look at her. They're wondering if she might be your—"

"Enough," Rafe growled, cutting him off. "What happens between Alana and me is none of their concern. The pack's safety is my only priority. Is that clear?"

Liam nodded, but his eyes held a mixture of sympathy and worry. "Crystal clear, Alpha." He left, closing the door softly behind him.

Alone once more, Rafe leaned against the wall, his forehead pressing against the cool surface. The weight of leadership bore down on him, threatening to crush him beneath its unyielding pressure. He closed his eyes, trying to center himself, but all he could see was Alana's face, her eyes wide with wonder and desire.

A memory surfaced, unbidden – his father's words on the day Rafe had become Alpha. "A leader's heart belongs to his pack, son. There's no room for selfish desires."

With a roar of frustration, Rafe slammed his fist into the wall, leaving a spiderweb of cracks in the plaster. He stared at the damage, his chest heaving, as blood trickled from his split knuckles.

A soft gasp drew his attention to the doorway. Alana stood there, a basket of herbs in her arms, her eyes wide as she took in the scene before her.

"I... I'm sorry," she stammered. "I heard a noise. I thought you might be hurt."

Rafe straightened, trying to compose himself. "It's nothing," he said gruffly, hiding his injured hand behind his back.

Alana set down her basket and approached him slowly, as one might a wounded animal. "Let me see," she said softly, holding out her hand.

For a moment, Rafe remained still, torn between his need to appear strong and his desperate desire for her touch. Finally, he relented, extending his bloodied hand.

Alana cradled his much larger hand in both of hers, her touch feather-light as she examined the wound. "This needs to be cleaned," she murmured, leading him to a nearby chair.

As she worked, gently cleaning and bandaging his hand, Rafe found himself mesmerized by her movements. The gentle press of her fingers, the warmth of her breath on his skin – each sensation sent shockwaves through his body.

"There," Alana said at last, her voice barely above a whisper. "All better."

Rafe looked down at his bandaged hand, then back at Alana. She was so close, her scent enveloping him, clouding his judgment. Without thinking, he reached out with his uninjured hand, cupping her cheek.

Alana leaned into his touch, her eyes fluttering closed. For a moment, the world fell away, leaving only the two of them, suspended in a bubble of shared longing.

The spell was broken by a howl in the distance – a summons from the council. Reality came crashing back, and Rafe jerked away as if burned.

"I have to go," he said roughly, standing abruptly. "Pack business."

Alana nodded, her eyes searching his face. "Rafe," she began, reaching for him.

He stepped back, his expression hardening. "Thank you for your assistance, healer," he said formally. "That will be all."

Hurt flashed across Alana's face before she schooled her features into a neutral mask. "Of course, Alpha," she replied, her voice cool. She gathered her herbs and left without another word.

As the door closed behind her, Rafe slumped back into the chair, his head in his hands. The beast within him raged, furious at being denied what it wanted most. But the Alpha in him knew he had made the right choice. His pack needed a leader, not a lovesick fool.

With a heavy heart, Rafe rose and prepared to face the council. He had a pack to protect, a war to prepare for. There was no room for weakness, no matter how badly his heart ached for what could never be.

As he strode out of his quarters, Rafe's resolve hardened. He would be the Alpha his pack needed, even if it meant sacrificing his own happiness. The image of Alana's hurt expression lingered in his mind, a painful reminder of the cost of his duty.

Little did he know, as he made his way to the council meeting, that forces were already in motion that would soon test his resolve to its very limits.

CHAPTER 6

*T*he ancient redwoods loomed overhead, their massive trunks disappearing into the mist that clung to their upper reaches. Alana followed Rafe through the forest, her footsteps silent on the carpet of pine needles. The air was thick with the scent of damp earth and decaying leaves, a rich, primordial aroma that seemed to pulse with hidden life.

Rafe moved with the fluid grace of a predator, his broad shoulders taut beneath his worn leather jacket. He led her deeper into the heart of the forest, away from the prying eyes and ears of the pack. The further they went, the more the silence seemed to press in around them, broken only by the occasional cry of a distant bird or the rustle of unseen creatures in the underbrush.

Finally, they emerged into a small clearing. At its center stood a massive redwood, its trunk easily twenty feet in diameter. Rafe approached it running his hand over the rough bark with a reverence that made Alana' breath catch in her throat.

"This is where it happened," Rafe said, his voice barely above a whisper. The words seemed to hang in the air, heavy with unspoken pain.

Alana stepped closer, drawn by the raw emotion in his voice. "What happened here, Rafe?"

He turned to face her, his hazel eyes clouded with memories. For a moment, he looked lost, vulnerable in a way that made Alana's heart ache. Then, as if steeling himself, he squared his shoulders and began to speak.

"Fifteen years ago, this clearing ran red with the blood of my family," he said, each word seeming to cost him dearly. "My father was Alpha then. We thought we were safe here, protected by the ancient trees and the spirits of our ancestors."

Rafe's hand clenched into a fist, his knuckles white with tension. "We were wrong."

As he spoke, the clearing around them seemed to shimmer, like heat rising from summer-baked asphalt. Alana blinked, and suddenly the scene had changed. The peaceful glade was gone, replaced by a nightmarish tableau of violence and terror.

Ghostly figures darted between the trees – snarling wolves with eyes that glowed red in the darkness. At the base of the great redwood, a massive silver wolf stood defiantly, teeth bared as it faced down a pack of shadowy assailants. Behind it cowered two smaller forms – a young boy and a little girl, their eyes wide with fear.

"The Shadow Pack came in the dead of night," Rafe continued, his voice distant, as if he too was seeing the phantom images. "They'd been growing bolder, pushing at our borders, but we never imagined they'd dare a full-scale attack."

The silver wolf lunged, tearing into the nearest attacker with savage fury. But for every enemy it felled, two more seemed to take its place.

"My father fought like a demon, but there were too many. He ordered me to run, to get my sister to safety." Rafe's voice cracked, the first tear sliding down his cheek. "I... I hesitated. Just for a moment. But it was enough."

The scene shifted again. Now Alana could see a younger Rafe, no more than fifteen, frozen in indecision as chaos erupted around him. His sister tugged at his arm, pleading with him to move.

A blood-curdling howl split the air, and the silver wolf stumbled, dark blood matting its fur. In that instant of distraction, a black wolf larger than any Alana had ever seen burst from the shadows. Its jaws closed around the throat of Rafe's sister, silencing her scream forever.

"No!" The anguished cry tore from Rafe's throat, echoed by his younger self in the vision. The clearing snapped back to its present-day tranquility, leaving Alana gasping and disoriented.

Rafe stood with his back to her, his shoulders shaking with silent sobs. Without thinking, Alana closed the distance between them, wrapping her arms around him from behind. She pressed her cheek against his back, feeling the rapid beat of his heart.

"It wasn't your fault," she whispered fiercely. "You were just a boy, Rafe."

He turned in her embrace, his eyes wild with a pain that seemed to transcend time. "I should have been faster, stronger. If I had just listened to my father..."

Alana reached up, cupping his face in her hands. "You survived," she said, willing him to believe her. "You lived to lead your pack, to protect them. Your father would be proud of the Alpha you've become."

For a long moment, Rafe stared at her, searching her face for something Alana couldn't name. Then, with a low growl that was more wolf than man, he crushed his lips to hers.

The kiss was desperate, hungry, fueled by years of pent-up grief and rage. Alana met his passion with her own, pouring all her compassion and understanding into the connection between them.

When they finally broke apart, both were breathing heavily. Rafe rested his forehead against hers, his eyes closed.

"The wolf who killed my sister," he said softly, "it was Zev. That's why I can never trust the Shadow Pack. Why I'll do anything to keep them from hurting anyone else I... care about."

Alana's heart raced at the implication in his words. She opened her mouth to respond, but a twig snapped in the forest beyond the clearing. In an instant, Rafe was on alert, pushing Alana behind him as he scanned the treeline.

"We should go," he said, his voice once again taking on the authoritative tone of the Alpha. "It's not safe to linger here."

As they made their way back to Whispering Falls, Alana's mind whirled with all she had learned. The weight of Rafe's past, the depth of his pain – it all served to deepen her resolve. Whatever challenges lay ahead, whatever dangers the Shadow Pack might pose, she knew now that she would face them at Rafe's side.

What neither of them realized, as they walked in contemplative silence, was that they had not been alone in the clearing. Hidden in the shadows of the ancient redwoods, Lysandra crouched, her eyes gleaming with malicious triumph. She had witnessed everything – Rafe's moment of vulnerability, the kiss that spoke volumes about his feelings for Alana.

As the Alpha and the healer disappeared from view, Lysandra slipped away in the opposite direction. She had information to share, and she knew just the wolf who would be very interested to hear it.

****

The journey back to Whispering Falls seemed to stretch on endlessly, the forest around them growing darker as twilight approached. Alana walked beside Rafe, close enough to feel the heat radiating from his body, yet separated by an invisible barrier of unspoken words and raw emotion.

As they neared the outskirts of the pack's territory, Rafe suddenly stopped, his hand shooting out to grasp Alana's arm. His nostrils flared as he scented the air, eyes narrowing as they scanned the deepening shadows between the trees.

"What is it?" Alana whispered, her heart rate quickening.

Rafe's grip on her arm tightened. "We're being followed," he growled, his voice low and dangerous.

In one fluid motion, he pulled Alana behind him, shielding her with his body as he faced the threat. A twig snapped in the underbrush, and a figure emerged from the gloom.

"At ease, Alpha," came a familiar voice. "It's only me."

Liam, Rafe's Beta, stepped into a patch of fading sunlight, his hands raised in a placating gesture. Rafe's posture relaxed slightly, but Alana could still feel the tension thrumming through him.

"What are you doing out here, Liam?" Rafe demanded, an edge of suspicion in his tone.

Liam's eyes flicked briefly to Alana before settling back on his Alpha. "There's been another incident at the border. The council is waiting for you."

Rafe cursed under his breath, running a hand through his hair in frustration. He turned to Alana, conflict evident in the set of his jaw. "I have to go," he said, his voice rough with barely contained emotion. "We'll finish this... conversation... later."

Before Alana could respond, Rafe had shifted, his human form blurring and reforming into that of a massive wolf with fur the color of burnished copper. With one last, intense look at Alana, he bounded off into the forest, Liam close on his heels.

Left alone in the gathering dusk, Alana wrapped her arms around herself, suddenly chilled despite the mild evening air. The weight of all she had learned pressed down on her, threatening to overwhelm her senses. She needed space to think, to process the raw pain she had witnessed in Rafe's eyes.

Almost without conscious thought, her feet carried her away from the path back to the village. She found herself drawn to a small stream that cut through the forest floor, its gentle burbling a soothing counterpoint to the tumult of her thoughts.

Alana knelt at the water's edge, trailing her fingers through the cool current. As she did so, a memory surfaced – a teaching from her adoptive father, the shaman who had raised her.

"Water holds memory," his voice echoed in her mind. "It carries the stories of all it has touched, from the highest mountain to the deepest sea."

Acting on instinct, Alana closed her eyes and reached out with her senses, not just to the water, but to the forest around her. She felt the ancient strength of the redwoods, the quiet rustle of small creatures in the underbrush, the whisper of wind through leaves high above.

And beneath it all, a current of something else – a wild, primal energy that seemed to pulse in time with her own heartbeat. It was the same energy she had felt when healing, but stronger here, more focused.

A twig snapped nearby, jolting Alana back to awareness. She opened her eyes to find herself surrounded by a small crowd of forest animals – a curious deer, a family of raccoons, even a majestic barn owl perched on a low-hanging branch. They watched her with an intelligence that went beyond mere animal instinct.

"Hello," Alana said softly, unsure of what else to do. To her amazement, the deer stepped forward, lowering its head to nuzzle gently at her hand.

A rush of images flooded her mind – flashes of the forest as seen through the eyes of its inhabitants. She saw the ebb and flow of seasons, the dance of predator and prey, the slow growth of saplings into towering giants. And threaded through it all, the presence of the wolves – guardians, protectors, a vital part of the forest's balance.

As the visions faded, Alana found her cheeks wet with tears she didn't remember shedding. She understood now, on a bone-deep level, what Rafe and his pack truly meant to this place. And she knew, with a certainty that both thrilled and terrified her, that her destiny was inexorably linked with theirs.

"Thank you," she whispered to the assembled creatures. One by one, they melted back into the forest, leaving Alana alone with her newfound resolve.

Rising to her feet, she turned back toward Whispering Falls, her steps purposeful. She had made her decision. Whatever challenges lay ahead, whatever dangers the Shadow Pack might pose, she would face them at Rafe's side. Not just for him, but for the pack, for the forest, for the delicate balance that she now understood she was a part of.

As she walked, Alana failed to notice the pair of gleaming eyes watching her from the shadows. Lysandra crouched low, her lip curling in a silent snarl as she observed the healer's determined stride. This new development would certainly interest Zev — and perhaps provide the leverage Lysandra needed to secure her own position of power.

With silent, predatory grace, Lysandra slipped away into the deepening night, her mind already racing with plans and possibilities. The game was changing, and she intended to be several moves ahead.

CHAPTER 7

The mist clung to the ancient redwoods like a lover's embrace, shrouding Whispering Falls in a veil of secrets. As night descended, Lysandra slipped through the shadows, her footfalls muffled by the damp forest floor. Her heart raced, not with fear, but with a heady cocktail of ambition and jealousy that coursed through her veins like liquid fire.

She paused, her keen senses alert for any sign of discovery. The waterfall's distant roar masked her movements, but she couldn't risk being seen. Not now, when she was so close to getting everything she'd ever wanted.

Lysandra's lips curled into a snarl as she thought of Alana, the outsider who'd bewitched not only the pack but their Alpha as well. *Rafe should be mine*, she thought, her claws extending involuntarily at the memory of his intense gaze fixed on the healer.

Reaching a small clearing, Lysandra withdrew a battered cell phone from her pocket. Its screen illuminated her face, casting eerie shadows across her beautiful features. She typed quickly, her fingers dancing across the keys as she composed her message to Zev, Alpha of the Shadow Pack.

The pack gathers for the full moon hunt tomorrow. Alana will be with the elders, learning our ways. The western border will be lightly guarded.

She hesitated for a moment, her thumb hovering over the send button. A flicker of doubt crept into her mind, but she quashed it ruthlessly. *This is for the good of the pack*, she told herself. *Rafe is too blinded by his infatuation to see the danger Alana poses.*

The message sent, disappearing into the ether with a soft chime. Lysandra allowed herself a small smile of triumph, imagining Zev's reaction. She could almost see his scarred face, twisted with cruel anticipation.

As she made her way back to the village, Lysandra's keen ears caught the sound of laughter drifting on the night air. She froze, melting into the shadows of a massive redwood. Through the mist, she saw them - Alana and Rafe, walking side by side along the moonlit path.

Alana's head was tilted back, her laughter like wind chimes in the breeze. Rafe watched her with an expression Lysandra had never seen before - open, unguarded, almost... vulnerable. The sight made her stomach churn.

"You're telling me you've never howled at the moon?" Rafe was saying, his deep voice tinged with amusement.

Alana shook her head, her eyes sparkling. "Never had the urge. But maybe you could teach me?"

Rafe's answering chuckle was low and intimate. "I'd be honored, little healer."

Lysandra's claws dug into the bark of the tree, leaving deep gouges. She watched as Rafe took Alana's hand, leading her towards the heart of the village. The tenderness in the gesture was unmistakable, and it made Lysandra's blood boil.

As their figures faded into the mist, Lysandra emerged from her hiding place. Her beautiful face was contorted with rage and jealousy, her eyes glowing with an almost feral light.

"Enjoy it while you can, *little healer*, she hissed into the darkness. *"Your time here is coming to an end."*

In the distance, a lone wolf howled - a mournful sound that seemed to echo Lysandra's tortured soul. She tilted her head back and joined the cry, pouring all her frustration and dark desires into the haunting melody.

As the sound faded, Lysandra squared her shoulders and headed back to the village. She had played her part; now, she would wait for the storm to break. And when it did, she would be there to pick up the pieces and claim her rightful place at Rafe's side.

The mist swirled around her retreating figure, as if nature itself was trying to wash away the stain of her betrayal. But some marks run too deep to ever truly fade, and the seeds of destruction Lysandra had sown would soon bear bitter fruit.

****

The early morning mist clung to Alana's skin as she made her way through the Redwood Pack's village, her footsteps light on the dew-dampened earth. The scent of pine and wild herbs filled her nostrils, a reminder of the natural world she'd always felt most at home in. As she approached the pack's nursery, a chorus of whimpers and yips reached her ears.

Pushing aside the heavy leather flap that served as a door, Alana stepped into the dimly lit interior. The air was thick with the musky scent of wolf pups and milk. In the corner, a young mother wolf lay curled around her litter, her eyes fever-bright and anxious.

"Shh, it's alright," Alana murmured, approaching slowly. She held out her hand, palm up, allowing the mother to catch her scent. "I'm here to help."

The wolf's ears flattened against her head, a low growl rumbling in her chest. Alana paused, then sank to her knees, making herself smaller. She began to hum softly, a melody as old as the forest itself. Gradually, the tension in the air dissipated.

With careful movements, Alana reached out to touch the mother wolf's flank. A warm glow emanated from her palm, seeping into the animal's body. The wolf's breathing eased, her eyes closing in relief.

"That's it," Alana whispered, her free hand gently stroking the pups. "You're doing so well."

A shadow fell across the entrance, and Alana looked up to see Rafe's imposing figure silhouetted against the morning light. His eyes, usually so guarded, softened as he took in the scene before him.

"How are they?" he asked, his deep voice barely above a whisper.

Alana smiled, her hand still resting on the mother wolf. "Much better now. The infection is clearing, and her milk should come in fully by nightfall."

Rafe nodded, a flicker of something – pride? admiration? – crossing his face. "You have a way with them that I've never seen before."

"It's nothing, really," Alana demurred, rising to her feet. "I just—"

Her words were cut short as a commotion erupted outside. Angry voices and the sound of breaking wood shattered the morning calm. Rafe was out the door in an instant, Alana close on his heels.

In the center of the village, two young wolves circled each other, teeth bared and hackles raised. A broken fence lay between them, splinters scattered across the ground.

"Enough!" Rafe's voice boomed across the clearing, the full weight of his Alpha authority behind it.

The two wolves froze, their heads lowering in submission. As they shifted back to human form, Alana recognized them as Jace and Kody, two of the pack's most promising young warriors.

"What is the meaning of this?" Rafe demanded, his eyes flashing with anger.

Jace, his chest heaving, pointed an accusing finger at Kody. "He said I was too weak to join the border patrol! That I'd put the whole pack at risk!"

Kody snarled, taking a step forward. "It's true! You can barely hold your wolf form for an hour!"

Rafe moved to intervene, but Alana laid a hand on his arm. "May I?" she asked softly.

After a moment's hesitation, Rafe nodded, curiosity evident in his expression.

Alana approached the two young wolves, her presence somehow both soothing and commanding. "Jace," she said, her voice gentle but firm. "Show me your hands."

Confused, Jace held out his hands. Angry red welts crisscrossed his palms, a testament to hours of gripping tree branches and rocks in wolf form.

Without a word, Alana took his hands in hers. That familiar warmth spread from her touch, and the welts began to fade before their eyes.

"You've been pushing yourself too hard," she said, meeting Jace's gaze. "Your body needs time to adjust, to grow stronger. It's not weakness to acknowledge your limits."

She turned to Kody, whose angry expression had given way to something closer to shame. "And you," Alana continued, "have forgotten that a pack is strongest when it supports all its members, not just the naturally gifted."

A hush had fallen over the gathered crowd. Even Rafe watched in silent amazement as Alana guided the two young wolves to clasp hands.

"Now," she said, her voice carrying across the clearing, "why don't you both join me in repairing this fence? There's much to be learned in working together."

As the three of them set to work, the tension in the air dissipated like morning mist. Rafe found himself staring at Alana, marveling at the way she'd defused the situation without a hint of supernatural compulsion. It was as if she'd tapped into something more fundamental – the very essence of what it meant to be pack.

From the shadows of a nearby hut, Lysandra watched the scene unfold, her nails digging crescents into her palms. She saw the way Rafe looked at Alana, the respect and something deeper shining in his eyes. It made her stomach churn.

Enjoy your moment in the sun, little healer, Lysandra thought bitterly. *It won't last much longer.*

As if sensing the malevolent gaze, Alana glanced up, her eyes scanning the crowd. For a brief moment, her gaze locked with Lysandra's, and a shiver ran down the healer's spine. But then Jace called for her attention, and the moment passed, leaving Alana to wonder at the strange sense of unease that had come over her.

The day wore on, and as the sun began to dip below the treeline, Alana found herself by the sacred pool at the heart of the Redwood Pack's territory. The water shimmered with an otherworldly light, reflecting the first stars of evening.

She knelt at the water's edge, her fingers trailing through the cool liquid. As she did so, a vision flashed before her eyes — wolves running through a moonlit forest, the sound of battle cries on the wind, and at the center of it all, a pair of mismatched eyes, one blue, one amber, filled with a hunger that made her blood run cold.

Alana jerked back, her heart pounding. She looked around wildly, but the clearing was empty save for the rustling leaves and the gentle lapping of the pool.

"What was that?" she whispered to herself, rubbing her arms to dispel the chill that had settled over her.

Unbeknownst to Alana, her innocent touch had set in motion events that would soon bring chaos to the Redwood Pack. The ripples spread outward from her fingertips, carrying whispers of prophecy and danger to those with the power to hear them.

And in the depths of the Shadow Pack's territory, Zev's mismatched eyes snapped open, a cruel smile spreading across his scarred face. "Soon," he growled, his voice thick with anticipation. "Very soon."

CHAPTER 8

*T*he forest was a living, breathing entity, its ancient redwoods standing sentinel as the Redwood Pack moved silently through the underbrush. Dappled sunlight filtered through the canopy, casting ever-shifting patterns on the forest floor. The air was thick with the scent of pine, damp earth, and the musky aroma of wolf.

Alana crouched behind a fallen log, her heart thundering in her chest. This was her first hunt with the pack, and despite her growing comfort among the werewolves, she felt like an intruder in this primal ritual. Beside her, Rafe's massive form was coiled with tension, his amber eyes scanning the clearing ahead.

"Remember," he whispered, his breath warm against her ear, "stay close and follow my lead."

Alana nodded, suppressing a shiver that had nothing to do with the cool forest air. Rafe's proximity sent sparks dancing along her skin, a reminder of the growing connection between them.

A twig snapped in the distance, and the entire pack froze. Through the trees, Alana caught a glimpse of tawny hide and proud antlers – a herd of elk, grazing peacefully in a sun-dappled meadow.

Rafe's muscles bunched, ready to spring. But before he could give the signal, a gust of wind swept through the clearing, carrying with it the unmistakable scent of wolf. The lead elk's head snapped up, nostrils flaring.

In an instant, the peaceful scene erupted into chaos. The elk bolted, their panicked bleats shattering the forest's tranquility. The pack burst from cover, a symphony of snarls and pounding paws as they gave chase.

Alana found herself swept up in the rush, her legs pumping as she struggled to keep pace. The world blurred around her, reduced to flashes of green and brown, the thundering of hooves, and the wild song of the hunt.

Suddenly, a young elk stumbled, its leg catching in a tangle of roots. It bleated in terror, thrashing wildly as the pack closed in. Alana's heart clenched at the raw fear in its eyes, so familiar to her own not so long ago.

Without thinking, she surged forward, outpacing even Rafe. As she neared the fallen elk, a strange calm washed over her. The forest seemed to hold its breath, the chaotic sounds of the hunt fading to a distant murmur.

Alana raised her hand, palm outward, and a soft, pulsing light emanated from her skin. Her voice, when she spoke, seemed to come from somewhere deep within the earth itself.

"*Hush now, little one,*" she crooned in a language as old as the forest. "*Be still. Be calm. You are safe.*"

The elk's thrashing slowed, its wild eyes fixing on Alana. The light from her palm seemed to envelop the creature, soothing its panic. With gentle movements, Alana approached, her free hand working to untangle the elk's leg.

"*There you go,*" she murmured. "*Run free, child of the forest.*"

As if understanding her words, the elk scrambled to its feet. It gave Alana one last, wondering look before bounding away, disappearing into the undergrowth.

The spell broken, Alana became aware of the stunned silence around her. She turned to find the entire pack staring at her, their expressions a mix of awe and wariness. Rafe stood at the forefront, his eyes wide with a cocktail of emotions Alana couldn't begin to decipher.

"Alana," he breathed, taking a step towards her. "What... what was that?"

She opened her mouth to respond, but no words came. The strange power that had flowed through her moments ago now left her feeling hollow and drained. The forest spun around her, the trees seeming to close in.

"I... I don't..." Alana stammered, her vision blurring. She swayed on her feet, and Rafe was there in an instant, his strong arms catching her before she could fall.

"It's okay," he murmured, though the tension in his voice belied his words. "I've got you."

As consciousness slipped away, Alana caught fragments of hushed conversation around her.

"Did you see her eyes?"

"...just like the legends..."

"...could she be the one?"

Then darkness claimed her, and she knew no more.

In the shadows of the forest, unseen by the preoccupied pack, a pair of mismatched eyes gleamed with triumph. Lysandra melted back into the underbrush, her mind racing with the implications of what she'd just witnessed.

Oh, little healer, she thought, a cruel smile twisting her beautiful features. *You've just made my job so much easier.*

As the Redwood Pack made their way back to Whispering Falls, Alana cradled unconscious in Rafe's arms, none of them noticed the lone wolf slipping away through the trees. Lysandra had a message to deliver, and Zev would be most interested in this latest development.

The hunt was over, but a far more dangerous game was just beginning.

****

The journey back to Whispering Falls was a blur of hushed whispers and furtive glances. Rafe cradled Alana's unconscious form against his chest, her warmth seeping through his shirt, a stark contrast to the chill that had settled in his bones. The forest, usually a comforting presence, now seemed to watch with wary eyes, as if it too sensed the shift in the air.

As they approached the village, Elder Elara emerged from her hut, her weathered face creased with concern. "Bring her here," she commanded, her voice brooking no argument.

Rafe ducked into the dimly lit interior, gently laying Alana on a bed of furs. His hands lingered for a moment, reluctant to break contact. Elara's knowing gaze bore into him, and he straightened, clearing his throat.

"What happened out there?" Elara asked, her gnarled hands already moving to examine Alana.

Rafe ran a hand through his hair, pacing the small space. "I... I'm not sure. The elk panicked, and Alana, she just..." He trailed off, the image of Alana suffused in that otherworldly light burning behind his eyelids.

Elara hummed, a sound that could have meant anything. "Her pulse is strong, her breathing steady. It seems she's merely exhausted."

"But what did she do?" Rafe's voice came out sharper than he intended. "I've never seen anything like it. The way she calmed that elk, the language she spoke... it was like..."

"Like she was one with the forest itself," Elara finished, her eyes glinting in the dim light.

Rafe nodded, a shiver running down his spine. "What does it mean, Elder? Is she... is she dangerous?"

The old woman's laughter filled the hut, rich and unexpected. "Oh, my boy. All power is dangerous in the wrong hands. The question is, are hers the right ones?"

Before Rafe could respond, a soft moan came from the bed. Alana stirred, her eyelids fluttering. Rafe was at her side in an instant, his large hand engulfing hers.

"Alana? Can you hear me?"

Her eyes opened, unfocused at first, then locking onto his face. For a moment, Rafe could have sworn he saw a flash of gold in their depths, gone so quickly he might have imagined it.

"Rafe?" Her voice was hoarse. "What... what happened?"

He exchanged a glance with Elara, who nodded almost imperceptibly. "What do you remember?" he asked gently.

Alana's brow furrowed. "The hunt... the elk..." Her eyes widened suddenly, and she sat up so abruptly that Rafe had to steady her. "The elk! Is it—"

"Safe," Rafe assured her, marveling at her concern for the creature they had been hunting. "Thanks to you."

A look of relief washed over her face, quickly replaced by confusion. "But how did I...? I don't understand what happened."

Rafe's thumb traced small circles on the back of her hand, a gesture meant to soothe them both. "Neither do we, exactly. But Alana, what you did out there... it was unlike anything I've ever seen."

She pulled away, wrapping her arms around herself. "I'm sorry, I didn't mean to interfere with the hunt. I just couldn't bear to see it suffer, and then it was like something took over, and—"

"Peace, child," Elara interrupted, her voice gentle but firm. "You've done nothing wrong. But I think it's time we had a talk about your gifts, and where they truly come from."

Rafe's eyes narrowed. "You know something about this, Elder?"

Elara sighed, suddenly looking every one of her many years. "I have... suspicions. Tales passed down through generations, whispers of a prophecy..."

A heavy silence fell over the hut. Outside, the normal sounds of pack life continued, oblivious to the tension within. Rafe's mind raced, pieces of a puzzle he hadn't known existed starting to fall into place. Alana's unique abilities, her connection to the forest, the way she had integrated so seamlessly into pack life despite being human – or so they had thought.

"What prophecy?" Alana's voice was barely above a whisper.

Elara moved to a ancient chest in the corner, retrieving a bundle wrapped in deerskin. With reverent hands, she unfolded it, revealing a piece of bark covered in intricate markings.

"Long ago," she began, her voice taking on a rhythmic cadence, "it was foretold that in our darkest hour, when the balance of nature itself was threatened, one would come who could bridge the gap between worlds. Neither fully human nor wolf, but something... more."

Rafe's gaze darted between the bark and Alana, whose face had gone pale. "Are you saying that Alana is...?"

"I'm saying nothing for certain," Elara cautioned. "But the signs are there for those with eyes to see."

Alana's hands trembled as she reached for the bark. The moment her fingers made contact, a soft glow emanated from the markings, pulsing in time with her heartbeat. She snatched her hand back with a gasp.

Rafe's protective instincts surged. He moved to stand between Alana and the artifact, his body tense. "Enough," he growled, a hint of his wolf bleeding into his voice. "This is too much, too soon. She needs rest, not riddles and ancient prophecies."

Elara regarded him coolly. "And what of the pack, Alpha? They saw what happened today. They'll have questions, fears. How will you address them?"

The weight of leadership settled heavily on Rafe's shoulders. He glanced at Alana, seeing the fear and confusion in her eyes, and made a decision.

"For now, we say nothing," he declared. "This stays between us until we understand more. I won't have rumors and speculation tearing the pack apart."

Elara nodded, though her expression suggested she had more to say on the matter. "As you wish, Alpha. But secrets have a way of revealing themselves, often at the most inopportune moments."

A howl pierced the air outside, signaling the return of a patrol. Rafe straightened, his duty calling.

"Rest," he told Alana softly. "We'll figure this out together, I promise."

As he turned to leave, Alana caught his hand. "Rafe," she said, her voice small. "Are you... afraid of me now?"

The vulnerability in her eyes tugged at something deep within him. Without thinking, he brought her hand to his lips, pressing a gentle kiss to her knuckles.

"Never," he whispered fiercely. "Whatever this means, whatever you are... you're pack. You're..." He trailed off, unable to voice the depth of his feelings.

Alana's eyes shimmered with unshed tears, but a small smile curved her lips. It was enough, for now.

As Rafe stepped out into the fading daylight, his mind whirled with the implications of what he'd learned. Prophecies, hidden powers, threats lurking in the shadows – the path ahead was fraught with danger. But as he glanced back at the hut where Alana rested, he felt a surge of determination.

Whatever storm was coming, they would weather it together.

CHAPTER 9

*T*he moon hung low and bloated in the inky sky, its pale light barely penetrating the thick canopy of Blackrock Ridge. In the heart of the Shadow Pack's territory, a figure stood silhouetted against the eerie glow. Zev, his scarred face a mask of determination, surveyed the gathering of his most trusted warriors.

The air crackled with anticipation, a low growl rumbling through the assembled werewolves. Zev's voice cut through the tension like a blade. "Brothers and sisters," he began, his words dripping with barely contained fury, "the time has come to claim what is rightfully ours."

His gaze swept across the crowd, amber eyes glowing with an unholy light. "For too long, we've watched our pack wither, our strength fade." He paused, letting the words sink in like poison. "But no more. Tonight, we take back our destiny."

A chorus of snarls and howls erupted, the pack's bloodlust rising like a tide. Zev allowed himself a cruel smile, the scar across his eye twisting grotesquely. "Our spy has given us the key," he continued, his voice dropping to a conspiratorial whisper. "The Redwood Pack harbors a treasure beyond measure – a healer with powers that could ensure our dominance for generations to come."

The name "Alana" rippled through the crowd like a shiver. Zev's fist clenched, nails elongating into deadly claws. "She is the answer to the prophecy, the salvation foretold by our ancestors. And tonight, we will rip her from Rafe's grasp and make her ours!"

As if on cue, a lithe figure emerged from the shadows. Lysandra, her beauty a sharp contrast to the savagery around her, approached Zev with feline grace. "My Alpha," she purred, her eyes gleaming with ambition, "I bring fresh news from Whispering Falls."

Zev's nostrils flared, drinking in the scent of betrayal that clung to Lysandra like a second skin. "Speak," he commanded, his voice a low growl.

Lysandra's lips curled into a satisfied smirk. "Their defenses are weakest near the eastern ridge," she reported, her words laced with the sweetness of revenge. "A small team could easily breach their perimeter there, creating a distraction while we strike at the heart of their territory."

Zev nodded, his mind already racing with possibilities. He turned back to his warriors, his voice rising to a fever pitch. "We strike at dawn!" he roared, eliciting a cacophony of howls. "Remember, Alana is to be taken alive. Her power is useless to us if she's dead."

As the pack dispersed to prepare, Zev pulled Lysandra aside. His claws traced the curve of her jaw, a gesture both intimate and threatening. "You've done well," he murmured, his breath hot against her ear. "When this is over, you'll have your reward. Rafe's pack will crumble, and you'll stand at my side as we usher in a new era for our kind."

Lysandra shivered, caught between desire and fear. "And what of Alana?" she asked, unable to keep the jealousy from her voice.

Zev's laugh was cold and mirthless. "She'll serve her purpose," he said dismissively. "But power, my dear Lysandra, that's the true aphrodisiac. And soon, we'll have more than we ever dreamed possible."

As the first hints of dawn began to bleed into the sky, the Shadow Pack moved like wraiths through the forest. The air was thick with the scent of impending violence, the very trees seeming to recoil from their passing. At their head, Zev's eyes gleamed with unholy anticipation. Soon, he thought, the healer would be his, and with her, the key to unimaginable power.

In the distance, shrouded in mist and blissfully unaware of the approaching storm, Whispering Falls slumbered on. But not for long. The peace of the Redwood Pack was about to be shattered, and at its center, Alana's world would be forever changed.

****

The pre-dawn mist clung to Whispering Falls like a ghostly shroud, muffling sounds and blurring shadows. Rafe stood atop the village's highest watchtower, his muscular frame taut with tension. His eyes, sharp as hawk's, scanned the surrounding forest. Something was off. The usual symphony of birdsong and rustling leaves had been replaced by an eerie silence.

A twig snapped in the distance. Rafe's head whipped around, nostrils flaring. The scent hit him like a physical blow – Shadow Pack. His lip curled into a snarl.

"Sound the alarm!" he roared, his voice echoing through the sleeping village. "Everyone to battle stations!"

The peaceful calm of Whispering Falls shattered. Wolves erupted from their homes, some already shifted, others struggling into clothes as they ran. Rafe leapt from the tower, landing with feline grace. He sprinted towards the village center, barking orders as he went.

"Liam!" he called to his Beta, who was already organizing a group of younger wolves. "Take a team to the eastern ridge. It's our weak point."

Liam nodded grimly. "On it, Alpha." He turned to his group. "You heard him! Move out!"

Rafe continued through the village, his presence both reassuring and galvanizing. He reached the healers' den, where Elara was hurriedly packing supplies.

"Elder," he said, his voice softening slightly. "We need to move the vulnerable to the safe caves. Can you oversee the evacuation?"

Elara's weathered face was a mask of determination. "Of course, Alpha. But what about Alana? She'll want to help."

As if summoned by her name, Alana appeared in the doorway, her eyes wide with concern. "Rafe, what's happening?"

Rafe's heart clenched at the sight of her, but he pushed the feeling aside. Now wasn't the time. "Shadow Pack," he said tersely. "They're coming. Alana, I need you to go with Elara. Your safety is paramount."

Alana's jaw set stubbornly. "No. I can help. My healing—"

"Is exactly why you need to be protected," Rafe cut her off, his voice brooking no argument. "Please, Alana. I can't fight if I'm worrying about you."

Something passed between them, an unspoken current of emotion. After a moment, Alana nodded reluctantly.

Satisfied, Rafe turned back to the chaos of the village. He spotted a group of warriors near the armory, struggling with a heavy wooden barricade.

"Put your backs into it!" he shouted, jogging over to lend his strength. Together, they heaved the massive structure into place, fortifying the village's main entrance.

A young wolf named Caleb approached, his face a mix of excitement and fear. "Alpha, what are my orders?"

Rafe clasped the boy's shoulder. "You're with me, Caleb. We're the last line of defense. If they breach the outer perimeter, we hold them here."

Caleb's chest swelled with pride. "Yes, Alpha!"

As the first rays of sunlight began to pierce the mist, Rafe climbed atop a large boulder in the village square. His voice rang out, clear and strong.

"Redwood Pack! Our home is threatened, but we are not afraid. We are strong. We are united. And we will not fall!"

A chorus of howls answered him, the sound rising to the heavens like a battle cry.

Rafe's eyes blazed with fierce determination. "Take your positions. Watch each other's backs. And remember — we fight not just for ourselves, but for our future. For our pack. For our home!"

As the pack dispersed to their assigned posts, Rafe allowed himself one last glance towards the healers' den. Alana stood in the doorway, her gaze locked on him. In that moment, unspoken words passed between them — a promise, a prayer, a declaration of something deeper than either dared to name.

Then the moment passed. Rafe turned away, his form shimmering as he shifted into his massive wolf form. He padded to the front lines, flanked by his most trusted warriors. The air crackled with tension, every wolf poised on a knife's edge between anticipation and dread.

In the distance, a lone howl pierced the dawn – the battle cry of the Shadow Pack. The Gathering Storm had arrived, and the fate of Whispering Falls hung in the balance.

CHAPTER 10

The moon hung low and heavy in the sky, its silvery light filtering through the dense canopy of the ancient redwoods. The air crackled with an ominous energy, as if the very forest held its breath in anticipation of the impending storm. In the heart of Whispering Falls, the Redwood Pack's sanctuary, an uneasy stillness settled over the village like a suffocating blanket.

Alana stood at the edge of the clearing, her senses on high alert. The night whispered dark secrets, and she could feel the forest's unrest prickling along her skin. Her green eyes, flecked with gold, scanned the treeline, searching for any sign of movement. The healer's fingers twitched, ready to channel her gift at a moment's notice.

Nearby, Rafe prowled the perimeter, his powerful form a symphony of barely contained strength and grace. His dark hair gleamed in the moonlight, and his eyes, usually a warm amber, now blazed with an inner fire. The Alpha's jaw was set in grim determination, his nostrils flaring as he scented the air.

"Something's wrong," Alana murmured, her voice barely above a whisper. "The animals... they're too quiet."

Rafe's gaze snapped to her, a mixture of concern and admiration flashing across his face. "Your connection to them grows stronger," he observed, moving closer. The heat of his body sent a shiver down Alana's spine, a stark contrast to the chill of foreboding that had settled in her bones.

Before either could speak again, a blood-curdling howl shattered the night's silence. It was a sound of rage, of hunger, of impending violence. Rafe's body tensed, a low growl rumbling in his chest. "Shadow Pack," he snarled, his features beginning to shift as the wolf within clawed its way to the surface.

As if summoned by their Alpha's fury, the Redwood Pack emerged from their homes, eyes glowing and claws extended. But even as they gathered, ready to defend their territory, chaos erupted from the forest's edge.

Dark shapes burst from the undergrowth, a tide of snarling fur and flashing fangs. The Shadow Pack had breached their defenses, their attack as swift and merciless as a lightning strike. At their head, a massive black wolf with a distinctive scar across one eye led the charge – Zev, his muzzle already stained with blood.

"How?" Rafe roared, his voice a mixture of disbelief and rage. "Our defenses—"

His words were cut short as the two packs collided in a maelstrom of tooth and claw. The clearing became a battleground, the air filled with snarls, yelps of pain, and the sickening sound of flesh tearing.

Alana's heart raced as she watched Rafe leap into the fray, his powerful jaws clamping down on the throat of a Shadow Pack warrior. All around her, the night exploded into violence. She knew her place wasn't in the thick of the fight, but her hands itched to help, to heal.

A pained cry drew her attention. To her left, a young Redwood wolf lay bleeding, his leg twisted at an unnatural angle. Without hesitation, Alana rushed to his side, her hands already glowing with the soft green light of her healing touch. As she worked, she felt the forest respond to her power, tendrils of energy seeping up through the earth to aid her efforts.

But even as she mended bones and sealed wounds, Alana couldn't shake the feeling that something was terribly wrong. The Shadow Pack's attack was too coordinated, too precise. They seemed to know exactly where to strike, as if...

A flash of golden hair caught her eye, and Alana's blood ran cold. Lysandra stood at the edge of the battle, her beautiful face twisted into a mask of triumph and malice. Their eyes met for a brief, terrible moment, and in that instant, Alana understood. The betrayal cut deeper than any physical wound, leaving her gasping for breath.

"Rafe!" she cried out, desperate to warn him. But her voice was lost in the cacophony of battle.

As if drawn by her distress, Zev's massive form materialized from the chaos. His mismatched eyes, one amber and one milky white, fixed on Alana with predatory intensity. "At last," he growled, his voice a guttural rumble that sent ice through her veins. "The healer is mine."

Alana scrambled backward, her heart pounding a frantic rhythm against her ribs. She could feel the raw power emanating from Zev, the weight of his ambition and desperation pressing down on her like a physical force. In that moment, faced with the enormity of the threat before her, Alana felt something stir deep within her soul – a power she had only glimpsed, now rising to meet the challenge.

The battle raged on around them, a tempest of fur and fang, but for Alana, time seemed to slow. She could hear Rafe's roar of fury as he fought to reach her, could sense the desperation of her pack as they struggled against the Shadow Pack's onslaught. And beneath it all, she felt the pulse of the earth, the whisper of ancient power that had always been a part of her.

As Zev lunged, jaws snapping, Alana made a choice. With a primal cry that echoed through the clearing, she embraced the wildness within her, feeling it surge through her veins like liquid fire. The world around her blurred, her body contorting and shifting in ways she had never experienced before.

In a flash of blinding light, where Alana once stood, a magnificent wolf now crouched – her fur a shimmering silver, her eyes blazing with emerald fire. The battle froze, all eyes turning to witness the impossible transformation.

Alana, the healer, had become the very thing she had been healing – a wolf powerful and untamed. And as she raised her head to meet Zev's stunned gaze, a howl of defiance tore from her throat, echoing through Whispering Falls and beyond, heralding a turning point in the war between the packs.

The night was far from over, and the true test of Alana's newfound power was only beginning.

****

Alana's paws barely touched the ground as she darted between the warring wolves, her newly transformed body a blur of silver fur. The coppery scent of blood filled her nostrils, threatening to overwhelm her senses. But she pushed through, driven by an instinct as old as time itself - to heal, to protect.

A pained whimper caught her attention. She skidded to a halt beside a fallen Redwood warrior, his flank torn open by vicious claws. Without hesitation, Alana pressed her muzzle against the wound, channeling her healing energy in a way she'd never done before. The wolf's flesh knitted together under her touch, the fur regaining its healthy sheen.

"By the moon," the warrior gasped, staggering to his feet. "How did you-"

But Alana was already gone, racing towards the next cry for help. Her mind reeled, struggling to process the chaos around her while grappling with her newfound form. Yet somehow, her healing touch seemed stronger, more focused than ever before.

Across the clearing, Rafe's thunderous roar rose above the din of battle. Alana's head snapped up, her heart clenching at the sight of her Alpha locked in fierce combat with Zev. The two massive wolves circled each other, fangs bared, neither willing to give an inch.

"You've grown soft, Rafe," Zev taunted, his scarred eye gleaming with malice. "Harboring strays, playing at peace. Your father would be ashamed."

Rafe's only response was a bone-chilling growl as he lunged, jaws snapping inches from Zev's throat. But the Shadow Alpha was quick, twisting away and countering with a vicious swipe of his claws.

Alana yearned to rush to Rafe's aid, but a desperate cry from nearby stopped her short. Elder Elara lay pinned beneath two snarling Shadow warriors, her wizened face contorted in pain. Without thinking, Alana leapt, her newfound strength propelling her through the air. She crashed into the attackers, sending them tumbling away from the Elder.

"Alana, child," Elara wheezed, her eyes wide with a mixture of awe and concern. "You must not exhaust yourself. Your power-"

"I can't stop," Alana interrupted, her voice a low rumble in her wolf form. "They need me. I can feel it, Elara. Every injury, every drop of blood spilled. I have to do something!"

The Elder's gaze sharpened, a flicker of understanding passing over her features. "Then do what you must, but be warned. Great power comes at great price."

Before Alana could respond, a chilling howl cut through the night. Lysandra stood atop a rocky outcropping, her golden fur stained red, her eyes wild with a manic glee. "For the Shadow Pack!" she cried, signaling to a group of hidden warriors.

In that moment, Alana saw the tide of battle shift. More Shadow wolves poured from the trees, fresh and hungry for the kill. The Redwood Pack, already weary from the initial assault, began to falter under the renewed attack.

Panic clawed at Alana's chest as she watched her newfound family being overwhelmed. Her gaze darted frantically around the battlefield, taking in the wounded, the dying, the desperate faces of those still fighting. This was more than just a battle for territory. It was a fight for survival, for everything the Redwood Pack held dear.

"It's not enough," she whispered, her voice trembling. "My healing... it's not enough."

As if in response to her despair, Alana felt something stir deep within her. A wellspring of power, vast and ancient, pulsing just beneath her skin. She closed her eyes, reaching for that hidden reservoir, knowing instinctively that tapping into it would change everything.

"Rafe," she called out, her voice carrying across the clearing with otherworldly resonance. "I need you to trust me."

The Alpha's head snapped towards her, his amber eyes locking with hers even as he fended off another of Zev's attacks. In that brief moment of connection, a lifetime of understanding passed between them. Rafe gave an almost imperceptible nod, his faith in her unwavering.

Taking a deep breath, Alana planted her paws firmly on the blood-soaked earth. She threw her head back and let out a howl that shook the very foundations of the forest. It was a sound of raw power, of nature itself rising to her call.

The battle around her seemed to freeze, all eyes drawn to the spectacle unfolding in their midst. Alana's fur began to glow, pulsing with an ethereal light that grew brighter with each passing second. Tendrils of energy seeped from the ground, wrapping around her like living vines.

"What is this magic?" Zev snarled, taking an involuntary step back.

But Alana barely heard him. Her world had narrowed to a single point of focus - the beating heart of the forest itself. With a final, desperate push, she unleashed the full force of her power.

A shockwave of pure healing energy exploded outward, washing over the battlefield in a tidal wave of light. Where it touched, wounds closed, bones mended, and strength returned. The Redwood Pack howled in unison, invigorated by this miraculous second wind.

As the light faded, Alana swayed on her feet, her legs trembling with exhaustion. The world spun around her, darkness creeping at the edges of her vision. She was vaguely aware of Rafe's warm presence suddenly beside her, his strong form supporting her as she struggled to remain conscious.

"Hold on, my love," his voice rumbled in her ear. "The tide has turned. You've given us a fighting chance."

Alana managed a weak nod before the darkness claimed her, the sounds of renewed battle fading into the distance. As she slipped into unconsciousness, one thought echoed in her mind - the battle for Whispering Falls was far from over, and the true test of her newfound powers had only just begun.

CHAPTER 11

The moon hung like a tarnished silver coin in the ink-black sky, its light struggling to pierce the veil of smoke that choked the air. Whispering Falls, once a sanctuary of peace, now writhed in the throes of battle. The night was alive with snarls, yelps, and the sickening crunch of bone meeting fang.

Alana's heart thundered in her chest, a frantic drumbeat echoing the chaos around her. Her hands, once instruments of gentle healing, now trembled with exhaustion and desperation. She had poured her gift into countless wounds, mending flesh and bone until her own strength wavered like a guttering candle.

The Redwood Pack was faltering.

Everywhere she looked, familiar faces contorted in pain and fear. Beta Liam, his russet fur matted with blood, limped badly as he fended off two snarling Shadow warriors. Young Caleb, the first wolf she had ever healed, lay motionless beneath the gnarled roots of an ancient redwood. And Rafe..

Alana's gaze locked onto the Alpha's powerful form as he battled at the heart of the fray. Rafe moved like living lightning, all coiled power and deadly grace. But even he couldn't stem the tide alone. For every Shadow wolf he struck down, two more seemed to materialize from the darkness.

"Rafe!" The cry tore from Alana's throat as she saw Zev, the battle-scarred Alpha of the Shadow Pack, circling for an opening.

Rafe's head snapped toward her voice, amber eyes blazing with a mixture of fury and desperation. In that split second of distraction, Zev struck.

The Shadow Alpha's massive form crashed into Rafe like an avalanche of midnight fur and razor-sharp claws. They tumbled across the blood-slicked grass, a tangle of snapping jaws and raking claws. Alana's breath caught in her throat as she saw a spray of crimson arc through the air.

"No!" The word emerged as barely more than a whisper, drowned out by the cacophony of battle. But the terror that gripped Alana's heart roared like a tsunami.

She lurched forward, her legs leaden with fatigue. The world seemed to slow, each moment stretching into eternity as she watched Rafe struggle beneath Zev's onslaught. The Redwood Alpha's movements were growing sluggish, his normally lustrous coat dulled by dirt and blood.

Zev's mismatched eyes, one amber and one milky white, found Alana through the chaos. His muzzle pulled back in a grotesque parody of a smile, baring fangs stained crimson with Rafe's lifeblood.

"Watch closely, little healer," the Shadow Alpha's voice grated like gravel in her mind. "Watch as I take everything from you."

As if to punctuate his taunt, Zev's jaws clamped down on Rafe's exposed throat. The Redwood Alpha's eyes widened, a choked whimper escaping him as he thrashed weakly against the killing blow.

Something snapped within Alana.

A dam had burst in her soul, releasing a flood of raw, primal energy she had never known existed. The world around her faded, replaced by a swirling vortex of sensation and instinct. She felt the pulse of the earth beneath her feet, the whisper of ancient magics in the wind, the beat of a thousand hearts – wolf and human alike – echoing in her bones.

Alana threw her head back and unleashed a howl that shook the very foundations of the forest. It was a sound of rage, of desperation, of love pushed to its breaking point. But more than that, it was a call to awakening.

The transformation hit her like a bolt of lightning. One moment she stood on two legs, the next she was falling forward as her body reshaped itself with impossible speed. Bones shifted and realigned, muscles stretched and reformed, and fur erupted from her skin in a cascade of shimmering silver.

Where Alana the healer had stood, now crouched a wolf of breathtaking majesty. Her coat gleamed like moonlight given form, shot through with streaks of pure starlight. Eyes that had once been a warm green now blazed with an inner fire, flecked with gold and brimming with ancient power.

The battlefield fell silent, all eyes drawn to the impossible sight before them. Even Zev, in his moment of triumph, faltered at the sheer raw energy emanating from Alana's new form.

Alana's first step forward sent tremors through the earth, tiny shoots of grass and wildflowers springing to life in her wake. Her second stride brought with it a gust of wind that carried the scent of renewal and hope. By her third pace, the very air around her seemed to shimmer with barely contained power.

"Impossible," Zev snarled, his voice a mixture of awe and fury. He released his grip on Rafe, hackles rising as he faced this new threat.

Alana paid him no heed. Her entire world had narrowed to Rafe's prone form, his chest rising and falling in shallow, labored breaths. She pressed her muzzle to his wounds, feeling the familiar surge of her healing gift. But now, amplified by her newfound power, it flowed like a river of liquid sunlight.

Rafe's eyes fluttered open, focusing on Alana with a mixture of wonder and disbelief. "You..." he managed to rasp, his voice thick with pain and something else – a dawning realization.

Before either of them could speak further, a furious roar split the air. Zev, shaking off his momentary stupor, launched himself at Alana with all the pent-up rage of a thwarted victor.

Alana spun to meet him, her new form moving with a grace and speed that defied belief. As the two wolves collided in mid-air, a shockwave of pure energy rippled outward, staggering friend and foe alike.

The battle for Whispering Falls had entered a new phase, and nothing would ever be the same again.

****

The forest held its breath.

Where moments ago the air had been thick with snarls and the clash of battle, now an eerie silence descended upon Whispering Falls. All eyes, friend and foe alike, were fixed upon the impossible sight before them.

Alana stood, a vision of lupine majesty, her silver fur shimmering with an otherworldly light. Each breath she took sent ripples of energy through the air, causing leaves to tremble and the very ground beneath her paws to hum with power.

Zev, the fearsome Alpha of the Shadow Pack, took an involuntary step backward. His mismatched eyes narrowed, darting between Alana and hi own warriors. "What trickery is this?" he growled, his voice a mixture of rage and poorly concealed fear.

Rafe, still prone on the blood-soaked earth, struggled to his feet. His amber eyes never left Alana's form, wide with a mixture of awe and dawning realization. "The prophecy," he whispered, his voice barely audible.

At the sound of Rafe's voice, Alana's head snapped towards him. For a heartbeat, uncertainty flickered in her gaze. She took a hesitant step forward, then froze, as if suddenly aware of the eyes upon her.

A low murmur began to ripple through the gathered wolves.

"Is it really her?"

"How is this possible?"

"The healer... a shifter?"

Lysandra's voice cut through the whispers, sharp and accusatory. "She's been lying to us all along! She's not even one of us!"

The words seemed to jolt Alana out of her stupor. She shook her head, as if trying to clear it, and then... she spoke. Her voice, rich and melodious even in this new form, echoed with an undercurrent of ancient power.

I... I didn't know," Alana said, her words carrying clearly despite coming from a lupine muzzle. "I swear it."

She turned, addressing the stunned Redwood Pack. "This power, this form... it's as new to me as it is to you. But I am still Alana. Still your healer. Still..." Her gaze locked with Rafe's. "Still loyal to this pack."

Rafe took a halting step towards her, his expression a storm of emotions. "Alana, I—"

But before he could finish, Zev's snarl cut through the moment. "Enough of this! Shifter, healer, whatever you are – you belong to the Shadow Pack now!" He lunged forward, claws extended.

In that split second, Alana's newfound instincts took over. She pivoted with impossible grace, meeting Zev's charge head-on. As they collided, a burst of energy exploded outward, knocking nearby wolves off their feet.

The two Alphas tumbled across the clearing, a blur of midnight black and shimmering silver. Alana's lack of experience was evident, but her raw power more than made up for it. Where Zev's claws raked, her fur seemed to deflect the blows. When his jaws snapped, she was always just out of reach.

"Stay back!" Rafe barked as members of both packs moved to intervene. "This is between them now."

Alana and Zev broke apart, circling each other warily. Zev's scarred muzzle pulled back in a snarl. "You think your parlor tricks make you a match for me, little healer? I've spent a lifetime honing my power!"

To demonstrate, he launched himself at her again, this time feinting left before striking from the right. His claws found purchase, drawing a thin line of blood along Alana's flank.

A collective gasp rose from the Redwood Pack. But Alana didn't flinch. Instead, her eyes began to glow with an inner fire. Where Zev's claws had struck, the wound sealed itself almost instantly, leaving not even a scar.

"You're right, Zev," Alana said, her voice steady despite the exertion. "I don't know how to fight. But I do know how to heal." A small, almost sad smile played across her lupine features. "And sometimes, that's more powerful than any claw or fang."

With those words, Alana planted her paws firmly on the ground. A pulse of energy radiated outward, causing the grass beneath her to sprout and bloom in a matter of seconds. The wave of vitality washed over the gathered wolves, mending minor wounds and rejuvenating weary muscles.

Zev stumbled, momentarily overwhelmed by the surge of life force. "What... what are you?" he demanded, a note of desperation creeping into his voice.

Alana stood tall, her form seeming to grow even more majestic. "I am what I've always been," she declared. "A healer. A protector. And now..." She glanced at Rafe, something unspoken passing between them. "Now, I am the guardian this pack needs."

The air crackled with tension as both packs waited to see what would happen next. Alana's transformation had upset the balance of power, and now, with this display of her abilities, the entire dynamic of the conflict had shifted.

Rafe limped to Alana's side, his strength visibly returning thanks to her healing wave. He addressed both packs, his voice carrying the weight of an Alpha's authority. "The battle ends here. Zev, take your pack and go. You've seen what Alana can do. Do you really want to test her further?"

Zev's eyes darted between Alana, Rafe, and his own battered warriors. For a moment, it seemed he might press the attack. But then, with a snarl of frustration, he backed away. "This isn't over," he growled. "The prophecy—"

"Will unfold as it's meant to," Alana interrupted, her voice firm. "But not tonight. Not like this."

With a final, hate-filled glare, Zev turned and loped into the shadows of the forest. One by one, the Shadow Pack melted away after their leader, leaving behind only the scent of blood and defeat.

As the last of their enemies disappeared, the Redwood Pack erupted in a cacophony of howls – relief, triumph, and no small amount of confusion mingling in the sound. But beneath it all ran an undercurrent of awe, all eyes continually drawn back to Alana's shimmering form.

As the first light of dawn began to creep over the horizon, painting the sky in hues of pink and gold, the Redwood Pack gathered around their Alpha and their healer-turned-guardian. The battle was over, but it was clear to all that a new chapter in their story was just beginning.

CHAPTER 12

The aftermath of Alana's earth-shattering howl hung in the air like a veil of mist, slowly dissipating to reveal the battered but unbroken Redwood Pack. Rafe, his midnight fur matted with blood and dirt, stood tall amidst the chaos. His golden eyes, once clouded with doubt, now blazed with a fierce pride as he gazed upon Alana.

She padded towards him, her silver coat shimmering in the pre-dawn light. Each step was deliberate, powerful, a clear testament to the strength that now coursed through her veins. As she approached, Rafe's massive form seemed to soften, his muscles relaxing from their battle-ready tension.

"Alana," he rumbled, his voice a mixture of awe and tenderness. "You... you're magnificent."

A low chuckle escaped her throat, a sound both familiar and strange in her new form. "And you're a mess, my Alpha," she replied, her tail swishing with amusement.

Around them, the pack began to stir. Whispers rippled through the crowd, a mixture of excitement and uncertainty. Rafe's ears twitched, catching fragments of conversation.

"...never seen anything like it..."

"...is she really one of us now?"

"...what does this mean for the pack?"

Rafe's hackles began to rise, a growl building in his chest. But before he could speak, Alana stepped forward, her presence commanding attention.

"Redwood Pack," she called out, her voice carrying across the clearing. "I know you have questions. I have them too. But right now, we have wounded to tend to and a territory to secure."

She turned to Rafe, their eyes meeting in a silent exchange of trust and understanding. He nodded, then raised his voice to address the pack.

"You heard your Luna," he barked, the title sending a ripple of surprise through the gathered wolves. "Liam, take a patrol and sweep the perimeter. Make sure the Shadow Pack has truly retreated. Elena, gather our healers and start treating the injured. The rest of you, help where you can."

As the pack dispersed to their tasks, Rafe turned back to Alana. "Luna," he said softly, testing the word on his tongue. "It suits you."

Alana's tail wagged slightly, but her eyes remained serious. "Rafe, I-"

A commotion from the edge of the clearing cut her off. Liam burst through the underbrush, his gray fur bristling with alarm.

"Alpha! Luna!" he panted. "We've found something. You need to see this."

Without hesitation, Rafe and Alana bounded after Liam, their paws eating up the ground in perfect synchronization. They weaved through the ancient redwoods, the forest a blur of shadow and mist around them.

Liam led them to a small glade, where a group of Redwood wolves stood in a tight circle, their hackles raised. As Rafe and Alana approached, the circle parted, revealing a sight that made even Rafe's battle-hardened heart skip a beat.

There, sprawled on the forest floor, lay Zev. The Shadow Pack Alpha's once-proud form was battered and broken, his breath coming in ragged gasps. But it was his eyes that truly shocked them - no longer filled with hatred and ambition, they now held only fear and desperation.

"Please," Zev wheezed, his gaze locking onto Alana. "Help... my pack. The prophecy... it's killing us."

Rafe snarled, taking a protective step in front of Alana. "Why should we believe anything you say? After all you've done?"

Alana placed a gentle paw on Rafe's flank, her touch instantly calming his rising anger. She moved forward, her eyes never leaving Zev's face.

"What prophecy?" she asked, her voice firm but not unkind.

Zev coughed, a trickle of blood staining his muzzle. "Ancient... curse. Our pack... fading. Needed... healer. You."

Understanding dawned in Alana's eyes. She turned to Rafe, her expression resolute. "We have to help them."

Rafe's jaw dropped. "Alana, you can't be serious. After everything-"

"I am serious," she interrupted, her voice carrying the weight of her newfound power. "This is bigger than our feud, Rafe. If what he's saying is true, an entire pack is suffering. We can't turn our backs on that."

For a long moment, Rafe was silent, his eyes searching Alana's face. Then, lowly, he nodded. "This is why you're our Luna," he said softly. "Your compassion... it's what our pack needs. What I need."

He turned to the gathered wolves, his voice ringing with authority. "Bring Zev back to the village. Treat his wounds. And send word to the Shadow Pack. Tell them... tell them the Redwood Pack offers a truce."

As the others moved to carry out his orders, Rafe and Alana stood side by side, their fur brushing. The first rays of dawn broke through the canopy, bathing them in golden light.

"Whatever comes next," Rafe murmured, "we face it together. Alpha and Luna."

Alana leaned into him, drawing strength from his presence. "Together," she agreed.

As they made their way back to Whispering Falls, leading their battered but unbroken pack, both Rafe and Alana knew that this was just the beginning. The true test of their leadership - and their love - lay ahead. But with the bond between them stronger than ever, they were ready to face whatever challenges the future might hold.

CHAPTER 13

The mist-shrouded battlefield of Whispering Falls lay eerily silent, the echoes of snarls and howls fading into the ancient redwoods. Alana, her silver fur stained with the rust of dried blood, padded through the aftermath, her newly awakened senses overwhelmed by the cacophony of scents - fear, pain, and something else. Something... wrong.

Her ears pricked at a rustle in the underbrush. A flash of golden fur. A familiar scent, tinged with... guilt?

"Lysandra?" Alana called out, her voice carrying a new authority that surprised even her. "Show yourself."

The bushes parted, revealing the she-wolf. Lysandra's once-proud form now seemed diminished, her tail tucked low, ears flattened against her skull. But her eyes... they burned with a mixture of defiance and desperation that sent a chill down Alana's spine.

"It's over, Lysandra," Alana said, taking a step forward. "The Shadow Pack is defeated. Whatever game you've been playing-"

A snarl ripped from Lysandra's throat, cutting Alana off. "Game? You think this was a game?" She lunged forward, teeth bared. "You know nothing of sacrifice, of what it takes to survive in this world!"

Alana sidestepped the attack, her newfound agility allowing her to move with fluid grace. "Then enlighten me," she growled, circling her opponent. "What could possibly justify betraying your own pack?"

Lysandra's laugh was a bitter, broken sound. "My pack? They stopped being my pack the moment you arrived. The outsider. The miracle healer." Her words dripped with venom. "Do you have any idea what it's like to be replaced? To watch everything you've worked for slip away?"

As they circled each other, the forest seemed to hold its breath. Shafts of moonlight pierced the canopy, casting dappled shadows across the forest floor. In the distance, the mournful howl of a lone wolf cut through the night.

"I gave Zev information," Lysandra spat, her confession bursting forth like a dam breaking. "I told him about our defenses, about your routines. thought... I thought if I proved my worth, there might be a place for me Somewhere I belonged."

Alana's heart clenched, a mixture of pity and anger warring within he "And how many of your packmates paid the price for your 'belonging'?" sh asked, her voice low and dangerous.

Before Lysandra could respond, a deep, rumbling growl announced Rafe's arrival. The Alpha's massive black form materialized from the shadows, his golden eyes blazing with fury.

"Traitor," he snarled, advancing on Lysandra with deadly intent.

"Rafe, wait!" Alana interceded, placing herself between the Alpha and the trembling she-wolf. "She needs to face the consequences, yes. But not like this."

Rafe's growl deepened, a sound that vibrated through the very earth. "She betrayed us, Alana. Her actions led to the deaths of our packmates. The law is clear."

Alana met his gaze, unwavering. In that moment, she was every inch the Luna, her presence radiating a calm authority that seemed to soothe the rage in Rafe's eyes.

"Then let the pack decide," she said softly. "Let justice be served in the light of day, not in the heat of battle."

For a long moment, tension crackled between them like lightning. Then, slowly, Rafe nodded. "Very well, Luna," he said, the use of her title sending a shiver down Alana's spine. "We'll bring her before the pack council."

As Rafe moved to restrain Lysandra, Alana caught a glimpse of something in the she-wolf's eyes. Beneath the fear and defiance, there was a flicker of... hope?

"Why?" Lysandra whispered, her voice barely audible. "Why show me mercy after what I've done?"

Alana leaned in close, her words meant for Lysandra alone. "Because everyone deserves a chance at redemption," she murmured. "Even you."

As they made their way back to the heart of Whispering Falls, the first light of dawn began to break over the horizon. The mist that had shrouded the forest began to lift, revealing a world forever changed by the night's events.

Alana walked beside Rafe, their fur occasionally brushing, a silent comfort in the face of the challenges that lay ahead. Behind them, Lysandra stumbled along, flanked by watchful pack members.

The path to redemption would be long and arduous, for Lysandra and for the pack as a whole. But as Alana gazed at the brightening sky, she felt a glimmer of hope. They had survived the night. They had faced betrayal and emerged stronger.

And whatever the future held, they would face it together.

****

The sun crested the horizon, painting the sky in hues of amber and crimson as the Redwood Pack gathered at the edge of Whispering Falls. Alana stood beside Rafe, their fur still matted with the night's battle, but their eyes blazing with determination. Before them, the pack assembled - a sea of fur in various shades, some bearing fresh wounds, others trembling with exhaustion.

Rafe's voice rumbled across the clearing, a low growl underlining his words. "Brothers, sisters... we've weathered betrayal from within and assault from without. But we stand here, unbroken."

A murmur rippled through the crowd, tails swishing and ears twitching.

"The Shadow Pack thinks us weak," Rafe continued, his hackles rising. "They believe Lysandra's treachery has left us vulnerable. Shall we prove them wrong?"

A chorus of snarls and barks answered him, the pack's energy palpable in the crisp morning air.

Alana stepped forward, her silver coat catching the early light like spun moonbeams. "We are more than tooth and claw," she called out, her voice carrying a hint of her newfound power. "We are family. We are strength. And together, we are unbreakable."

As if summoned by her words, a haunting howl pierced the air. From the mist-shrouded forest emerged the Shadow Pack, their dark forms slinking between the ancient redwoods. At their head prowled Zev, his scarred face twisted in a snarl of anticipation.

"Last chance, Rafe," Zev called out, his voice dripping with false sympathy. "Hand over the healer, and we'll leave your little pack in peace."

Rafe's answering growl shook the very ground. "You'll have to go through all of us first."

Zev's laugh was cold and cruel. "Gladly."

With a bone-chilling howl, the Shadow Pack surged forward. But this time, the Redwood Pack was ready.

Alana felt a surge of pride as she watched her packmates spring into action. There was Liam, the loyal beta, leading a flanking maneuver with deadly precision. Elena, her healing skills rivaling Alana's own, darted between injured wolves, her touch bringing renewed strength.

And at the center of it all was Rafe, a whirlwind of midnight fur and flashing fangs. He met Zev head-on, the two alphas locked in a battle that seemed to shake the very forest.

Alana didn't hesitate. She leapt into the fray, her newfound agility allowing her to dance between friend and foe. Where her teeth found purchase, wounds appeared. Where her claws raked, fur parted like water.

But it was more than mere physical prowess that turned the tide. With each opponent she felled, Alana felt a pulse of energy ripple outward. Th

Redwood Pack, inspired by her courage and fueled by her power, fought with renewed ferocity.

"Push them back!" Rafe's voice boomed over the chaos. "For our home! For our future!"

The Redwood Pack answered with a deafening chorus of howls. They moved as one, a relentless tide of fur and fang that drove the Shadow Pack backward.

Zev, his arrogance giving way to disbelief, found himself suddenly isolated. His packmates, faced with the unified strength of the Redwood wolves, began to falter and retreat.

"Stand and fight, you cowards!" Zev snarled, but his words fell on deaf ears.

Alana and Rafe advanced on him, moving in perfect synchronization. Zev's eyes darted between them, a flicker of fear finally breaking through his mask of bravado.

"It's over, Zev," Alana said, her voice firm but not unkind. "Call off your pack. End this madness."

For a moment, it seemed as though Zev might lunge at them, choosing to go down fighting. But then, with a snarl of frustration, he threw back his head and let out a long, mournful howl.

At the sound, the remaining Shadow Pack wolves disengaged, slinking back into the misty forest. Zev fixed Alana and Rafe with a glare of pure hatred.

"This isn't over," he growled. "The prophecy-"

"Will be faced on our terms," Rafe interrupted, his voice brooking no argument. "Now go. Before we change our minds about letting you leave."

With a final, venomous look, Zev turned and melted into the shadows, leaving behind only the echoes of his retreating pawsteps.

As the last of the Shadow Pack disappeared, a stunned silence fell over Whispering Falls. Then, slowly at first but building to a crescendo, the Redwood Pack began to howl. It was a sound of triumph, of relief, of unity.

Alana felt the vibrations of it in her very bones. She turned to Rafe, seeing her own mix of exhaustion and exhilaration mirrored in his golden eyes.

"We did it," she breathed, her tail wagging despite her weariness.

Rafe nuzzled her gently, his voice a low rumble. "No, Luna. You did it. You united us. You showed us our strength."

As the pack's howls faded into tired but happy yips and barks, Alana gazed out over their battered but unbroken family. The dawn light filtered through the redwoods, casting dappled shadows across fur of every hue.

They had weathered betrayal. They had faced their enemies. And they had emerged stronger than ever.

But as Alana's gaze drifted to the misty forest where Zev had disappeared, she couldn't shake the feeling that this victory was just the beginning. The prophecy, whatever it might hold, still loomed on the horizon.

For now, though, they had earned their moment of peace. Tomorrow would bring new challenges. But they would face them together, as a pack, as a family.

United and unbreakable.

CHAPTER 14

*D*awn crept through the mist-laden branches of the ancient redwoods, painting the devastated clearing of Whispering Falls in hues of amber and gold. The air still carried the metallic tang of blood and the acrid remnants of battle, but beneath it stirred something new — the fresh, green scent of healing and renewal.

Alana moved among the wounded like a ghost, her bare feet silent on the dew-dampened earth. Her white dress, now stained with mud and blood, billowed in the morning breeze as she knelt beside each injured pack member. The silver threads of her healing power sparkled in her wake, weaving between the makeshift cots like starlight caught in a spider's web.

"Easy now," she murmured to Devon, a young warrior whose chest bore three savage claw marks. Her hands hovered over his wounds, emanating a soft, pulsing light. "Let the earth's energy flow through you."

The injured wolf whimpered, then sighed as his flesh began to knit together under her touch. Around them, other pack members watched with mixture of awe and lingering wariness. The revelation of her true nature — her ability to shift — still hung heavy in the air like thunder before a storm.

Rafe observed from the shadows of the great oak that housed the pack's meeting hall, his massive frame leaning against the weathered trunk. His amber eyes never left Alana, tracking her movements with an intensity that made the air between them crackle with unspoken words. The bandage across his torso was a stark reminder of how close they'd come to losing everything.

"She's something else, isn't she?" Elder Elara materialized beside him, her silver hair gleaming in the early light. "The prophecy spoke true."

Rafe's jaw tightened. "The prophecy nearly got her killed. Got us all killed."

"The prophecy," Elara corrected gently, "brought us our salvation. Look around you, Alpha. Our pack isn't just surviving — it's transforming."

Indeed, the scene before them was unlike anything the Redwood Pack had witnessed in generations. Wolves who had once been rivals now worked side by side, passing bandages and water, sharing stories of the battle. The hierarchy that had once divided them seemed to dissolve in the face of their shared victory and loss.

Alana finished with Devon and straightened, swaying slightly. Immediately, Rafe was there, his strong arms steadying her. The touch sent electricity coursing through both of them, their bond humming with recognition and need.

"You need to rest," he growled softly, his breath warm against her ear.

She turned in his embrace, her violet eyes meeting his amber ones. "There are still others who need healing."

"And they'll receive it after you've recovered your strength." His voice carried the weight of an Alpha command, but his touch remained gentle as he brushed a strand of silver-streaked hair from her face. "You're no good to anyone if you collapse."

A commotion at the edge of the clearing drew their attention. Two scouts dragged forward a struggling figure – Lysandra, her once-perfect features twisted with defeat and rage.

"We found her trying to slip away through the northern border," one of the scouts reported.

The clearing fell silent as Rafe and Alana approached the traitor. Lysandra refused to meet their eyes, her gaze fixed on the ground.

"Look at me," Rafe commanded, his Alpha power rolling through the clearing like thunder.

Lysandra's head snapped up, tears streaming down her face. "I only wanted—"

"To belong?" Alana stepped forward, her voice soft but carrying. "To feel powerful? There was always a place for you here, Lysandra. You just couldn't see it through your jealousy."

"The pack has spoken," Rafe declared, his voice heavy with judgment. "You are banished from Redwood territory. If you return, your life is forfeit."

As the scouts led Lysandra away, Alana leaned into Rafe's warmth, feeling the weight of the past days settle over her like a cloak. Around them, the pack began to move with renewed purpose — clearing debris, reinforcing defenses, preparing for whatever challenges lay ahead.

"What happens now?" she whispered, more to herself than to him.

Rafe's arms tightened around her. "Now, my Luna, we face the prophecy together. Whatever it holds, whatever comes next, we face it as one."

The morning mist began to lift, revealing glimpses of blue sky above the ancient redwoods. In the distance, a wolf howled — a song of mourning for what was lost, but also of hope for what was to come. One by one, other voices joined in, until the forest rang with their unified chorus.

Alana closed her eyes, feeling the power of the pack flow through her like a river finding its true course. She was no longer the outsider, the healer seeking refuge. She was Luna of the Redwood Pack, bound to these wolves and this forest by something stronger than prophecy — by choice, by love, by destiny freely embraced.

And as the sun rose higher, burning away the last shadows of battle, she knew that whatever challenges the prophecy might bring, they would face them together, stronger for having been broken, wiser for having known fear, and unshakeable in their unity.

The healing had begun, not just of bodies, but of hearts and bonds and ancient wounds. And in that healing lay the true power of the prophecy – not in the magic that flowed through Alana's veins, but in the transformation it had wrought in all of them, turning strangers into family, weakness into strength, and fear into hope.

****

Moonlight filtered through the ancient stained glass windows of Elder Elara's sanctuary, casting prismatic shadows across the worn stone floor. Centuries-old grimoires and scrolls littered the circular chamber, their pages rustling in the night breeze like whispered secrets.

Alana sat cross-legged in the center of a complex sigil etched into the floor, her silver-streaked hair gleaming in the candlelight. Sweat beaded on her forehead as she held her hands over a withered plant, willing life back into its branches.

"Focus," Elder Elara's voice cut through the silence. "Don't just heal – feel the connection. Your power flows from the earth itself."

The plant's stem began to straighten, green spreading through its leaves like watercolor bleeding across paper. Suddenly, the renewal accelerated — branches shooting upward, buds bursting into flowers, roots cracking through their pot.

"Stop!" Rafe's command cracked through the air as he lunged forward. The plant's growth froze, leaving a twisted, overgrown mass of vegetation.

Alana's hands dropped to her lap, trembling. "I can't control it. It's like trying to direct a river with my bare hands."

"The prophecy speaks of 'power unbound by moon or blood,'" Elder Elara shuffled through an ancient text, her gnarled fingers tracing the faded words. "Your abilities transcend traditional pack magic. You're not just healing — you're channeling life itself."

Rafe paced the chamber's perimeter, his boots silent on the stone. "And that's exactly why Zev won't stop hunting her. He'll rebuild his forces, gather allies. The Shadow Pack won't stay defeated for long."

"Then we need to be ready." Alana rose, brushing dirt from her jeans. She crossed to a massive oak table where a map of pack territories lay spread beneath crystalline paperweights. "Show me again where the ley lines converge."

Elder Elara hobbled over, placing gnarled fingers on specific points. "Here, beneath the Mirror Lakes. Here, at Raven's Point. And the strongest—"

"Directly beneath Whispering Falls," Rafe finished, coming to stand behind Alana. His presence radiated warmth against her back. "It's why our pack has held this territory for generations."

"And why the Shadow Pack wants it so badly." Alana traced the intersecting lines. "But there's something else. These patterns... they remind me of something my mentor used to—"

A howl pierced the night – urgent, alarmed. Rafe was already moving, his body tensing for transformation.

"Beta Liam," he growled. "Something's wrong."

They burst from the sanctuary into the cool night air. Pack members emerged from their homes, faces turned toward the northern border. Alana's heightened senses caught the acrid scent of fear carried on the breeze.

Liam materialized from the shadows, his clothes disheveled. "Alpha, Luna – we found something at the boundary stones. Something... wrong."

The trek to the border was tense, silent except for the whisper of leaves overhead. As they approached the ancient stones that marked pack territory, Alana's power began to hum beneath her skin, responding to... something.

"There." Liam pointed to the nearest boundary stone.

Carved into the weathered granite was a fresh symbol – a crescent moon bisected by a jagged line, dripping with what Alana's senses told her was blood. Shadow Pack blood.

"A warning?" she asked, reaching toward the mark.

Rafe caught her wrist. "Don't touch it. Dark magic leaves traces."

Elder Elara shuffled forward, her eyes narrowing. "Not just a warning. A claim. See how the line breaks the moon? It's an ancient symbol of prophecy rejection – a declaration of war against fate itself."

"Zev's response to the prophecy," Rafe's voice was deadly quiet. "He's declaring that if he can't have its power..."

"Then he'll destroy it." Alana finished, her hand finding Rafe's. "He'll try to destroy me."

The boundary stone seemed to pulse in the moonlight, the bloody symbol a promise of violence to come. But as Alana stood between her Alpha and their pack's elder, she felt something else pulse as well – power, yes, but also certainty. Purpose.

"Then we'll have to master the prophecy first." She turned to Elder Elara. "Teach me everything. Every ritual, every secret, every scrap of lore. No more holding back."

The old wolf's eyes glittered. "The teachings are dangerous, child. The old magics demand their price."

"I'll pay it." Alana's voice carried across the clearing, strong and sure. Around them, pack members emerged from the trees, drawn by her words. "We all will, if we must. But I won't let Zev's fear destroy everything we've built."

Rafe's hand tightened around hers. Through their bond, she felt his pride, his concern, his fierce love. "Whatever you need, Luna. The pack stands with you."

Elder Elara nodded slowly, her expression grave. "Then we begin tonight. Under the dark moon's watch, we'll unlock the secrets your mentor left buried in your blood." She turned to the gathered pack. "Prepare the sacred circle. Tonight, we embrace the prophecy's true power – all of it."

As the pack dispersed to make preparations, Alana stayed rooted before the boundary stone, studying the bloody symbol. In its crude lines, she saw not just Zev's defiance, but his fear. And in that fear lay opportunity – if she was strong enough to seize it.

"Ready?" Rafe's question rumbled against her ear.

Alana squared her shoulders, feeling the magic spark beneath her skin like lightning seeking ground. "Ready."

Above them, clouds scudded across the moon, and in the distance, a storm began to gather. The prophecy's next chapter was about to unfold, written not in ancient scrolls, but in power and blood and choice. And this time, Alana would be holding the pen.

CHAPTER 15

*T*he ancient redwoods whispered secrets to the dawn, their towering silhouettes piercing the morning mist like sentinels guarding the sacred grounds of Whispering Falls. Dew-kissed ferns unfurled beneath their branches, and the first rays of sunlight painted the forest floor in dappled gold, as if nature itself was celebrating this moment.

Alana stood at the edge of the ceremonial clearing, her bare feet rooted to earth still fresh with morning dew. The white dress she wore – woven with threads of silver and adorned with symbols of both her shamanic heritage and her new pack – caught the light like captured starfire. At her throat, the ceremonial pendant of the Luna gleamed, its surface etched with the very prophecy that had brought her to this moment.

"The signs are aligned," Elder Elara murmured, her gnarled fingers tracing patterns in the air. "The earth, the sky, the very magic in our blood – all speak of change."

From the shadows of the trees emerged the pack, moving in perfect formation. Young and old, warrior and healer, each carried a stone from th sacred circle where Alana had first discovered her true power. The stones gleamed with an inner light, responding to her presence.

Rafe appeared at the head of the gathering, his powerful frame clothed in the traditional garb of the Alpha – dark leather and silver, marked with the symbols of his lineage. The scars from their recent battle with the Shadow Pack were still visible on his chest, a testament to their struggles and victories.

Their eyes met across the clearing, and the bond between them surged like a live wire. Without words, they moved toward each other, drawn by something deeper than destiny.

"The pack gathers," Beta Liam called out, his voice carrying across the clearing. "To witness the dawn of a new era."

The circle formed naturally around them, stones being placed one by one in an intricate pattern that mirrored the constellation overhead. Each placement sent ripples of energy through the ground, making the very air hum with potential.

"For generations," Rafe's voice rolled across the gathering like thunder, "our pack has guarded these lands, guided by tradition and strength." His hand found Alana's, their fingers intertwining. "But today, we embrace something new – a power born of healing, not hatred. Of unity, not division."

Alana stepped forward, and the very forest seemed to lean in to listen. "I came to you as a stranger, carrying secrets and shadows." Her free hand rose, and with it, threads of silver light began to dance between the placed stones. "But you gave me more than shelter – you gave me purpose. Family. Home."

The magic building in the clearing responded to her words, sending sparks of energy spiraling upward through the morning mist. The pack members gasped as their own stones began to pulse in rhythm with their hearts.

"The prophecy spoke of power unbound," Elder Elara intoned, stepping into the circle. "Of healing that would transform, of love that would transcend the old ways." She placed her hands over their joined ones. "But prophecies are not chains to bind us – they are doors to open."

Rafe turned to face Alana fully, his amber eyes reflecting the dancing lights around them. "My father taught me that an Alpha's strength lies in his ability to protect." His voice roughened. "But you taught me that true strength lies in the courage to change, to trust, to love despite fear."

The energy in the clearing crescendoed as they began to move, circling each other in the ancient dance of wolf-mates. Each step left trails of light in their wake, weaving patterns that matched the prophecy stones buried beneath their feet.

"The Shadow Pack sought to possess this power," Alana spoke, her voice carrying to every corner of the gathering. "But true power cannot be taken – it must be shared." With each word, the silver light spread, touching each pack member in turn, creating a web of connection that sparkled in the morning air.

The dance brought them closer, their movements perfectly synchronized. Around them, the pack began to shift — not into their wolf forms, but into something in between, their eyes gleaming with shared power, their voices rising in the ancient songs of their people.

"I choose you," Rafe's words were for Alana alone, yet they seemed to echo through the very trees. "Not because of prophecy or power, but because of who you are — healer, warrior, mate."

"And I choose you," Alana answered, their faces now inches apart. "Alpha, protector, the other half of my soul."

As their lips met, the magic peaked. Light exploded outward from the circle, racing through the forest like liquid silver. Every stone in the circle blazed like a star brought to earth. The very ground beneath their feet thrummed with power.

Through their bond, Alana felt it all — Rafe's fierce love, the pack's unwavering loyalty, the ancient magic of the land itself responding to their union. But more than that, she felt the future unfurling before them like a path lined with possibility.

The kiss ended, but the magic didn't fade. Instead, it settled into the earth, into their bones, into the very fabric of their pack bonds — stronger, deeper, transformed.

"The dawn breaks," Elder Elara announced, her voice thick with emotion. "And with it, a new chapter begins."

The pack's howl rose as one — not a challenge or a call to battle, but a celebration of unity, of family, of love that had overcome darkness. The sound echoed through the ancient redwoods, carrying their story to the very stars that had foretold it.

And as the sun climbed higher, painting the world in shades of promise, Alana and Rafe stood together at the center of it all — Alpha and Luna, healer and protector, two souls bound by choice rather than fate. The prophecy that had brought them together was fulfilled, but their story was far from over.

It was, in truth, just beginning.

****

Firelight danced against the twilight sky, casting golden shadows across the faces of the gathered pack. The celebration fire roared at the center of Whispering Falls' clearing, its flames reaching toward stars that sparkled like scattered diamonds across the velvet night. The air thrummed with the beating of drums, their rhythm matching the pulse of the earth beneath their feet.

"Remember when you first stumbled into our territory?" Beta Liam raised his cup, droplets of mead catching the firelight. "Half-dead and still managing to heal that injured fox?"

Alana laughed, leaning back against Rafe's chest as they sat on the carved wooden throne that generations of Alphas had occupied. "I remember you nearly taking my head off before realizing I wasn't a threat."

"To be fair," Rafe's chest rumbled against her back, "you did cross our borders without permission." His fingers traced the Luna's pendant at her throat. "Best trespasser we ever caught."

Around the fire, pack members moved in the ancient dance of their people, bodies shifting fluidly between human and wolf forms. Young Cubs darted between the dancers' legs, their laughter mixing with the music. Near the feast tables, Elder Elara held court, regaling younger pack members with tales of prophecies past.

"Alpha! Luna!" Young Sarah, one of the Cubs Alana had healed during the Shadow Pack's attack, bounded up to their seat. "Watch what I learned!" The girl's form shimmered, and where she stood appeared a wolf pup with silver-tipped fur – a mirror of Alana's own wolf form.

"Impressive control," Rafe nodded approvingly. "You've been practicing."

"Luna Alana's been teaching me!" Sarah shifted back, bouncing on her toes. "She says our healing magic grows stronger when we embrace both sides of ourselves."

"Speaking of both sides," Beta Liam interrupted, gesturing toward the tree line. "Look who finally decided to join us."

Through the shadows walked the border patrol, but they weren't alone. With them came representatives from neighboring packs – even a few faces from packs that had once been hostile. Each carried traditional gifts: rare herbs, ceremonial weapons, scrolls of ancient lore.

"The Northern Alps Pack offers tribute to the Redwood Alpha and Luna," declared a warrior with frost-white hair. "And requests the honor of learning your healing ways."

Alana rose, her silver-embroidered dress catching the firelight. "The Redwood Pack welcomes you not as students or supplicants, but as equals." She descended the dais, touching each gift with fingers that sparked with silver light. "What was once hoarded will now be shared. What was once used to divide will now unite."

The visiting wolves bowed, then broke into grins as pack members pulled them toward the feast tables. Soon, ancient enemies shared mead and swapped stories like old friends.

"You've changed everything," Rafe murmured, coming to stand beside her. "Not just our pack, but the entire shifter world."

Before Alana could respond, a howl pierced the night – not of warning or war, but of joy. One by one, others joined in, the sound building until it seemed to shake the very stars. Wolves of different packs, different bloodlines, different traditions, all raising their voices in harmony.

"Dance with me," Alana turned to Rafe, her eyes reflecting the firelight. "Like we did when you first showed me what it meant to be pack."

They moved to the edge of the fire, and the circles of dancers parted for them. The drums picked up tempo, and Alana's feet moved to their rhythm, her body swaying like a flame in the wind. Rafe matched her step for step, their movements telling the story of their journey – from suspicion to trust, from fear to love, from division to unity.

Other couples joined them, and soon the clearing was a whirl of motion and magic. Silver sparks of healing energy danced between the revelers, responding to the joy in their hearts. Even the ancient redwoods seemed to sway to the music, their branches casting ever-changing shadows on the dancers below.

As the moon reached its peak, Elder Elara called for silence. The drums faded, the dancers stilled, and all eyes turned to the aged healer.

"For generations, we lived in fear of the prophecy," her voice carried across the hushed gathering. "We thought it foretold our end. Instead," she raised her gnarled hands toward Alana and Rafe, "it showed us our beginning."

The Alpha and Luna stood together, their silhouettes cast against the great fire behind them. Without words, they shifted in perfect unison – Rafe's massive black wolf form and Alana's silver one standing proud before their people.

The gathered packs erupted in cheers and howls. The drums began again, faster now, wilder. Cubs shifted and tumbled in play-fights, their parents watching indulgently. Warriors who had once fought each other now shared battle stories and drinking songs.

And through it all, two wolves – one black as night, one silver as starlight – moved among their people, touching noses with Cubs, accepting scratches from elders, their tails entwined. Where they walked, the very ground seemed to pulse with life, small flowers sprouting in their pawprints.

As the celebration continued under the star-filled sky, the prophecy stones buried beneath Whispering Falls pulsed with power – not of war or dominance, but of healing, of unity, of love. The age of division was over. A new dawn had truly begun.

And in the shadows of the ancient forest, watched over by trees that had seen centuries pass, the Redwood Pack celebrated not just their survival, but their transformation. They celebrated not just their Alpha and Luna, but the bonds that made them family. They celebrated not just the end of one story, but the beginning of countless more.

For in the end, that was what pack truly meant – not just surviving together, but living, loving, and growing together. Under the light of the same moon that had witnessed their struggles and triumphs, they were finally, truly, home.

EPILOGUE

The redwood forest bloomed out of season, wildflowers carpeting paths where two wolves ran beneath a waxing moon. Silver and black fur flashed between ancient trunks, their movements a dance as old as the earth itself. Where their paws touched ground, tiny sparks of healing energy sank into the soil, leaving trails of luminescent fungi and fresh growth in their wake.

At the sacred pool beneath Whispering Falls, the wolves shifted. Alana's bare feet settled on moss-covered stones, her silver-streaked hair catching moonlight like spun crystal. The leather-bound journal – her last link to the shaman who had raised her – rested in her hands, its pages finally complete.

"They're coming." Rafe's arms slipped around her waist, his chin resting on her shoulder. In the pool's reflection, his eyes held starlight. "The Northern Pack crosses our borders at dawn."

"Not as enemies this time." Alana traced the journal's worn cover, feeling the pulse of old magic beneath her fingertips. "Their Alpha's youngest daughter shows signs of healing gifts. Just like the other three we've discovered this moon cycle."

A splash drew their attention. In the shallow edges of the pool, three wolf cubs played – their fur a mixture of midnight and starlight. The smallest, a female with distinctive silver markings around her eyes, successfully pinned her larger brother.

"Just like her mother," Rafe chuckled as their daughter shifted to human form, her triumphant grin missing two front teeth.

"Papa!" Luna Sarah called out, water dripping from her silver-black hair. "I did it! I held the healing energy while shifting, just like Mama taught me!"

Her brothers shifted too, shaking water from their hair. "Show off," Marcus grumbled, but his eyes shone with pride for his sister.

The night air suddenly crackled with energy. Elder Elara emerged from the shadows of the ancient trees, her gnarled hands clutching a scroll that pulsed with familiar power.

"It's happening again," she announced, her voice carrying ancient weight. "The prophecy stones speak of more to come. More healers awakening, more packs transforming." Her wise eyes found Alana's. "Your guardian saw this day, child. It's all here, in the final pages he wrote before..."

13

Alana opened the journal to its last entry, written in the shaman's blood on the night he died protecting her. Words she couldn't read as a child now blazed with crystal clarity:

*When silver blood runs true and strong,

Through veins of those once lost to hate,

The ancient powers shall return,

And healing magic seal their fate.

Not one, but many shall arise,

From packs long torn by tooth and claw,

Till wolf-kind learns to mend its ways,

And peace becomes the highest law.*

"He knew," Alana whispered, remembering the fierce pride in his eyes that final night. "He knew I wouldn't be the only one."

A howl pierced the night — Beta Liam's signal. On the outskirts of their territory, the Northern Pack approached. Not with weapons or warriors, but with gifts and a child who needed guidance.

"Come on, cubs," Rafe called to their children. "Time to welcome our guests."

The children scrambled from the pool, shifting effortlessly between forms as they raced through the trees. Their laughter echoed like music through the ancient forest.

Alana placed the journal on a stone beside the falls, watching moonlight dance across its worn surface. Beyond the clearing, she could feel the pulse of ley lines running deep beneath the earth – the same lines that had guided her here years ago. They hummed stronger now, awakening after centuries of silence.

"Having second thoughts about training another healer?" Rafe's fingers entwined with hers, warm and sure.

Alana turned to face him, reaching up to trace the scar above his heart – a reminder of battles won and shadows overcome. "No," she smiled. "Having thoughts about how proud my guardian would be. He didn't die to keep this power hidden. He died so it could spread, grow, transform."

Their pack's howl rose through the night – a welcome call to their approaching guests. In that sound lived everything they'd built: strength tempered by compassion, power guided by wisdom, love strong enough to heal generations of hatred.

"Shall we?" Rafe's body began to shift, his black fur gleaming in the moonlight.

Alana cast one last look at the journal before letting her own transformation flow. Silver fur rippled across her skin as she took her wo— form, feeling the familiar surge of healing energy course through her veins.

Together, they raced through their territory, past the boundary stones now carved with symbols of peace rather than warnings. Past the training grounds where young healers would soon learn to embrace their gifts. Past the ancient redwoods that had witnessed their love story unfold.

The prophecy that had once threatened to tear their world apart had become a promise of renewal. The power that others had sought to possess had transformed into a gift freely given. And the love that had begun with a wounded healer and a haunted Alpha had become a beacon of hope for all wolf-kind.

As they crested the final ridge, the future sprawled before them like an unwritten page. But this time, they would write it together – not in blood or battle, but in healing, in teaching, in love passed down through generations yet to come.

The dawn of their new era had only just begun.

www.ingramcontent.com/pod-product-compliance
Lightning Source LLC
LaVergne TN
LVHW010716280425
809777LV00034BA/1146